GRATITUDE OF THE OCEAN

AND FIVE ADDITIONAL STORIES IN THE JOLENE TOMBERLIN SERIES

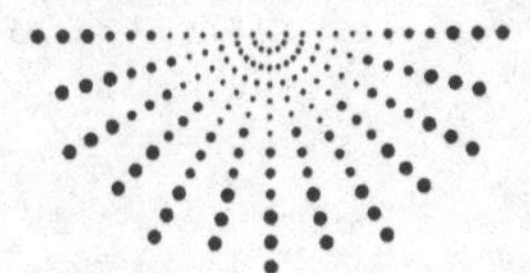

STEPHANNIE TALLENT

This is a work of fiction. Names, characters, places, and incidents either are the product of the author's imagination or are used fictitiously. Any resemblance to actual persons, living or dead, events, or locales is entirely coincidental.

Copyright © 2021 by Stephannie Tallent

All rights reserved.
No part of this book may be reproduced or used in any manner without written permission of the copyright owner except for the use of quotations in a book review.

For more information, contact: stephannie@stephannietallent.com

First e-Book edition July 2021

ebook ISBN: 978-1-942655-23-7
Print ISBN: 978-1-942655-24-4

www.stephannietallent.com

To Melanie, the sister of my heart

*The heart of man is very much like the sea, it has its storms, it has its
tides and in its depths it has its pearls too.*

—VINCENT VAN GOGH, **THE LETTERS OF VINCENT
VAN GOGH**

CONTENTS

INTRODUCTION

Jolene Tomberlin is one of my favorite characters. She's resourceful and smart, and has a soft spot for animals.

This collection includes my first Jolene stories.

It also includes a couple stories set in the past in the same just-a-step-sideways world.

The Little Animals, the Vermin, of Venice features some of Jolene's relatives in WWII Italy. The Seduction of the Sea takes place in early the 1900s in Carmel, California.

GRATITUDE OF THE OCEAN

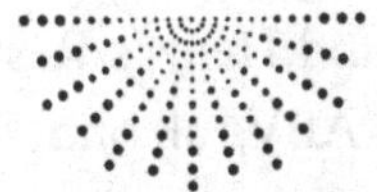

$\mathcal{A}$ rat, brown fur glistening in the moonlight, squeaked at Jolene as she tore the POLICE LINE tape loose and ducked under the half opened, half listing roll up garage door into the remains of the burned brick and steel warehouse.

"Git," Jolene said to it. "I'll talk to you later."

She hoped the roll-up door wouldn't crash down upon her. Shoot, she was praying the tar paper, charred plywood and scorched girders that made up the remnants of the roof stayed up where it belonged.

At least long enough for her to do a quick search.

Slagged glassware crunched under the soles of her leather and canvas combat boots. The smell of wood fire and flame retardant snuck past the surgical mask she wore.

Her sneeze echoed against the wall opposite the entrance.

Well, if there was anyone else lurking, they knew she was here. Nothing to do about it now.

The rat scrabbled at her pants leg. She sighed and picked it up, letting it nestle under her thick blonde braid, tucked under the collar of her black denim jacket. Rats got a bad rep, but she liked the little creatures.

"Best not have fleas, hon," she said to it. Its whiskers tickled her ear as it snuffled, raising the hair on the back of her neck. Messing with her ears always did that.

The warehouse *had* housed a craft brewery, Heart's Rest Brewing, one of many breweries setting up shop in the industrial area on the north side of Torrance, where rents were cheaper and you could have a couple food trucks in the parking lot.

She'd tried it once, a month or two after it opened last fall, with reservations. She liked to sip on barrel aged beers that packed a wallop of taste and booze, and Heart's Rest primarily featured easy to quaff, uncomplicated, low ABV, alcohol by volume, ales that were barely a step up from supermarket piss.

One beer had stood out, though: their barrel aged Black Shark Diving imperial stout, rich with an unusual spicy chocolate bitterness, so strange and complex and tasty that she'd had a full pour. She'd never had anything like it before, or since. They must've been working on that for awhile, to have it ready for the first month of opening. A small sign, hand printed and nailed to the wall under the chalkboard listing the beers, the price, and the ABV, alcohol by volume, noted there were more barrel aged brews on the way.

But she'd never gone back. She'd picked up a bit of food poisoning somewhere that day, puking her guts out all night, and irrational or not, the thought of drinking any more of their beer twisted her stomach even now.

Regardless, the space had been hipster trendy, with reclaimed wood tables and benches, and a bar that stretched halfway down one side, with a poured-concrete counter top. Games and magazines had filled a short bookcase on the opposite wall. Baskets of snacks: gourmet chicharrones, artisanal bison jerky, small batch sourdough pretzels, giving the patrons something to snack on if a food truck wasn't there. Large brewing tanks had filled the back half of the warehouse, filling the air with the rich scents of hops and yeast and malt. Steel rectangular frames with panes of old wavy glass fronted the warehouse on either side of the roll up garage door that served as the entrance.

Galen Veld, the brewer/owner, seemed like a nice guy, too. She'd met him once before he hired her, at a Rotary meeting last fall.

He'd caught her eye right off: scruffy long blond hair bound in a man bun at the nape of his neck, light blue eyes, surfer's moderately muscled build, all packaged self-consciously into a white button-down shirt and khakis she'd figured he'd bought for the meeting. She'd dragged herself there to drum up private investigation business, hating the necessity, forcing herself into black trousers with a cut three years out of date and a navy, black and cream flowered silk tank she'd bought at 90% off at Nordstrom Rack. They had chitchatted politely about beer and investigatory work.

Apparently her effort had paid off. He'd kept her card, and after the police had decided a couple days ago that the brewery caught fire by accident, from a faulty breaker, Galen hired her to find out what really happened.

Jolene had two skills passed on from her Dolly Parton-loving granny in East Texas that most private investigators lacked: the ability to communicate with animals, the little ones that lived amongst humans, what rude folks called vermin, and the Sense, the ability to see, smell or hear traces of magic. To step *down*, or *sideways*, and see what was there on the other side.

She didn't advertise either, but word got around the community. At least for those who knew about alternate realities, all the things that went bump in the night if only you could just see or hear or smell them.

Jolene scanned the scorched interior with normal human vision, stroking the rat's soft fur.

She wanted to see what the brewery looked like without the Sense, first.

The concrete bar was split into multiple pieces atop the remnants of the wooden base. The bookcase with the magazines and games was a sodden pile. Heaps of charred wood filled the space formerly occupied by the tables and benches. Moonlight streamed in through the broken front windows and the gaping hole in the roof.

Back in the far half of the brewery, in the dimness, the brewing tanks appeared scorched but intact. Jolene wondered if they could be refurbished. She bet they were expensive.

Nothing she wouldn't expect from a terrible fire.

She sighed, closed her eyes, concentrated, and went *down*.

No sight, no smell, no hearing. She couldn't even feel the weight or warmth of the rat on her shoulder.

Jolene hated this. She never felt more vulnerable during the few seconds it took to access the Sense, and she didn't do vulnerable. Despite her petite build, despite looking like a blue-eyed, blonde-haired California beach bunny, she taught women's self defense classes, had earned a black belt in Krav Maga, and could hit the red center circle of a target with a 9mm every freaking time.

Well, this was why she charged the big bucks.

When she opened her eyes, the world was different: darker, more jagged, scintillating. Darkness roiled near the brewing tanks, and the stench of rotting fish and thick brine assaulted her. A deep bass beat repeatedly kicked her in the gut; waves pounding upon the shore, ceaseless, impersonal. The little rat quivered upon her shoulder with each surge, paws entangled in her braid to help keep itself steady.

The room darkened, the chilly moonlight blocked by something, darkened til the only lights were phosphorescent flakes drifting through the air, like she'd dove into the abyssal depths.

Holy Mary Mother of God. Oh yeah, Galen was right. This was so not normal. Way more, way *deeper*, than she usually saw or felt or heard when she used the Sense.

The only reason she could think of for the perp using fire was the ocean was several miles away, too far for a tsunami or kraken to be used to destroy the brewery.

And seriously, that would be overkill and more than a bit obvious.

A slurping, slithery sound from behind the brewing tanks caused her to straighten in alarm, eyes widening to pick out anything in the darkness.

Not alone, then. At least not on this side.

The little rat had gone rigid with fear. She didn't know what the rat could sense, what he could smell or hear, but he obviously recognized a predator.

Time to go. She was paid for information, not for risking her life.

She closed her eyes. Just the darkness of her lids and flickers of light impulses from her retinas. *Up.*

The briny smell disappeared. *Up.*

The wet scraping sound came closer and closer, breaking her concentration.

Phosphorescence flickered beyond her closed eyelids. She tasted a hint of sweet rot. Felt the touch of a slimy tentacle upon her wrist. Heard the panicked squeak of the rat.

UP! Just darkness, and silence, and numbness in her nose and mouth, and her ragged breathing pulling her back to the real world.

She opened her eyes. The burned brewery, soft moonlight again streaming through the hole in the roof, was cozy in comparison to the water-logged *other* reality.

A bit of sticky slime coated the shoulder of her jacket and her braid.

The little rat was gone.

SHE SLUMPED against the red sticky vinyl of the booth of the all-night diner, shredding a paper napkin into long strips, ignoring her cooling coffee in its chipped ceramic mug. The moon had set, and it was closer to dawn than midnight, but she had decided she had to tell Galen what she'd learned ASAP.

The man had enemies with a capital E.

He slid into the booth opposite hers, dressed in faded ripped jeans and a Russian River Brewing t-shirt. His pale blue eyes were bloodshot.

"Hon, you have some scary folks with a heapload of hurt out for you," she said. No use sugar coating the news. She told him about the darkness, the waves, and the creature. Didn't tell him about the poor little rat. None of his business.

"So, merfolk, sirens, selkies," she concluded. "Or maybe someone else, someone older. That was a lot of power washing over me."

He looked away. "I have no idea who it could be," he said.

She sighed. Liar. She closed her eyes, shifted just a little, more *sideways* than *down*, then re-opened them.

Sure enough, Galen wasn't human. Least not completely. If she'd been as smart as she thought she was, she would've checked at their first meeting. Well, maybe not at the Rotary club meeting (now wouldn't that be interesting, seeing who was who?), but a day ago, when he hired her.

That scruffy blond hair? Sleek silver, a liquid metallic cloak trailing over his shoulders and so long he could nearly sit on it. Those pale blue eyes? Gleaming like aquamarines, set into a refined tanned face, the irises formed of fractal crystals of color, the effect inhuman but gorgeous. Those surfer muscles? Well, those were the same, and still nicely encased by the t-shirt and jeans.

"What are you?" she asked. Likely Sidhe, likely noble, every girl's dream faerie prince.

"None of your business," he said. He pulled his wallet out, extracted a stack of bills. "That should cover your fee. Thank you for your help, but I no longer require your assistance." He shoved the cash across the table to her and stood up.

"Wow. I think I deserve to know if that thing, or whoever set it there to guard or whatever, is going to come after me." She squinted. The money was real, not dried up leaves disguised as legal tender.

"They shouldn't."

"Thought you didn't know who it was."

"Goodbye, Miss Tomberlin." He stood.

Jerk. Prettier than a speckled pup, but who cared. Jerk.

"Got any more of that Black Shark?" she asked. "Some bottles stored elsewhere?"

Just a hunch. Sometimes she got them, and when she did, she'd learned to follow up.

He stiffened, then left.

~

TWENTY MINUTES later she was pulling her baby blue and rust Chevy Nova into her parking space in the underground garage for her apartment building. Parking in the South Bay was at a premium, especially if an ocean view came with the property, like her third floor condo did. Worth the extra bucks given her odd hours, to have a safe and consistent parking spot.

Brininess overwhelmed her as she exited her car into the dimly lit garage.

The stink of salt and fish wasn't unusual, given the location on the sand dune right inland and above the Redondo Beach Pier.

She loved the funkiness of the pier, with the old arcade with skee ball and vintage stand up video games, the various fish and crab restaurants, and the t-shirt and shell shops. Her favorite craft beer bar, all uncomfortable stools, rickety tables, and sticky concrete and linoleum floors, but with the draft list to end all draft lists, was down there too, tucked into the northeast corner of the u-shaped marina section.

The pier smelled a bit stale and rank, of old fried fish, cotton candy, and coconut sunscreen. Touristy, but like *Lost Boys* Santa Carla, a la Santa Cruz. 1980s. She loved that it wasn't gentrified to the point of blandness like so many beach towns.

But this stench was way more than usual, for even the hottest muggiest summer day, let alone the cool spring pre-dawn hours.

She felt the lurch and pull of an icy undertow around her feet, up her calves, reaching and grasping. She tasted bitter salt, painful on her tongue. Ocean spray slashed against her bare face. The garage was a sea cave, dank and dark and rocky. Treacherous. She touched the bit of slime on her jacket shoulder.

Still damp. That poor little rat. She shuddered and closed her eyes. *UP! UP! UP!*

But she hadn't invoked the Sense.

This had come to her, seeking her, lurking in wait for her.

There was no place for her to go.

She clenched her fists, shuffled one foot back, balanced herself, poised to launch an attack, and opened her eyes.

A thin figure, at least a foot taller than her five foot six, cloaked in a murky green hooded robe that swirled like seaweed in a riptide, stood quietly just out of arm's reach in front of her. He? She? tossed back their hood, wet greenish black hair trailing over their shoulders, accentuating the fish belly paleness of their skin.

Their face was angular, cheekbones sharp as the edge of a mussel shell, with lambent eyes, orange as the Garibaldi swimming in the kelp forest. Their white skin shimmered with a soft rainbow iridescence.

Beautiful. No wonder sailors gladly drowned for creatures like this.

And more terrifying than a nest of rattlesnakes.

"You sprung my trap," they said, their voice the shusharrah of windswept sand. "Meant for the despoiler. Why?"

"The despoiler?" said Jolene. "Galen?"

"He killed my children. Used them. Their fear, their deaths." The creature shuddered, stepped closer, close enough to lean in and sniff at Jolene, a ridge of scales on either side of their flat nose lighting up like a ctenophore then fading.

"You've tasted them," they said, thin lips pulling back in a grimace, exposing rows of shark-like teeth.

Jolene held herself rigid. Show no fear, show no fear. "I didn't know. I still don't kn--"

The beer. The Black Shark. That richness she'd never tasted before, the spiciness, the complexity. No. Oh no. How sick she'd been afterwards, but how good it has tasted.

"I'm so sorry." She ducked her head down, genuinely remorseful, making herself vulnerable. Hoping this inhuman creature had more mercy than that pretty two-headed snake of a Sidhe.

A claw-tipped finger under her chin, raising her head. She met those glowing orange eyes steadfastly.

"Can you lead me to him?" the creature asked. "I erred. When I destroyed the brewery, his place of torture, I erased all traces of *him*. I had hoped he would return himself, not send a proxy. Coward."

"I just have a phone number. We met at a coffee house."

They cocked their head. "I can hire *you* to find him. That is what you do, correct? Find things?"

Jolene nodded. "One of the things. But, wait -- you can track, right? That's how you found me, from the --" she stopped herself from saying slime "--the moistness from your beast?"

"My cousin," they said stiffly.

She dug in her pocket, withdrew the stack of bills. "Can you get Galen's scent from this? He just touched it, only a few hours ago."

Those orange eyes brightened. "I can." They took the bills and inhaled deeply. "Yes. Yessss." They yanked the hood up over their head, then the garage was empty except for parked cars and Jolene. No sea cave, no undertow, no spray on her face.

Just a strand of kelp laying across the hood of her car.

She left it there. A reminder.

~

SHE CRACKED open a bottle of barrel aged Imperial stout. No chocolate, no coffee, just rich thick maltiness. Meant for sipping, but she guzzled her first glass.

Sad about the creature's children. About the little rat.

Angry at Galen, but more angry at herself, for not fully checking him out, for trusting him. Burning a building seemed like such a rotten thing to do to someone.

Obviously, there were much worse things.

She finished the bottle, all 750 mls of 18% ABV, rather than capping it for the next day, then went to bed.

She twisted herself up in sweat-damp sheets, dreaming of sharks and stingrays, Garibaldi and moray eels, dolphins and sea lions, swimming free, living their lives, then being caught and tortured, those lives cut short.

SHE DECIDED to go to the farmer's market. It closed at 1 pm, the vendors packing up swiftly, but she would have about an hour to shop. Going to the market, then cooking a meal with fresh ingredients, grounded her.

Her granny always told her a home cooked meal could settle the heart.

Her heart desperately needed some settling.

The market was crowded, but she had her favorite vendors. Fresh asparagus, pea tendrils, radishes, all went into her bag. Some Valencia oranges, a pound of Ojai Pixie tangerines.

Her cell rang. Galen's number. She hesitated, then answered, steering herself out of the crowd, heading between two booths towards the packed parking lot.

"You bitch, what have you done?" Galen said.

He wasn't just furious. He was scared. For a moment Jolene let herself savor that fear, tasting an echo of the Black Shark Diving brew.

Then let it go.

"I gave them your blood money," she said.

"Do you know what they'll do to me?!"

"I suspect. Nothing you don't deserve, nothing worse than what you did. Better run, Galen, run so far inland that the vengeful sea can't find you."

JOLENE DIPPED a spoon into the pureed asparagus soup, tasted it. Delicious. Rich and bright and earthy, all at the same time. Pure.

She dished herself out a bowl of soup, topped it with a hefty spoonful of buttery toasted breadcrumbs, then a drizzle of creme fraiche, and a pinch of chopped chives cut fresh from the pot of herbs on her balcony. Poured herself a glass of St. Bernardus Tripel.

Grabbed a piece of sourdough she'd picked up at the market and a pat of salted butter for it.

Perfection.

She carted it all to her balcony to watch the sunset over the Pacific, hoping to see a green flash along the horizon.

The brininess in the air was soft, unthreatening, as the sun sank, kissing the horizon then dipping below.

And....yes! the green flash, brightening the sky for a scant second.

Her cell rang. Galen's number. Her stomach clenched. So much for a nice homemade dinner.

"Hello?"

"It is done," a soft voice like sand across the boardwalk. "Thank you, Jolene Tomberlin. My children are avenged. You have my gratitude."

"I --" she said, but they had hung up. Their gratitude. Precious, to be sure...but if Galen had kin, she was in a heap of trouble.

Maybe she should've thought of that before giving the sea creature the cash. She didn't think she would've done any different.

Nothing to do about it now. Tomorrow was another -- well, everyone knew that line.

Jolene finished her soup, enjoying the caress of sea spray on her face.

THE LOVE OF THE SEA

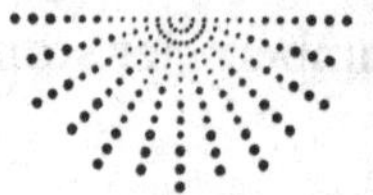

*B*rine-scented fog rolled in along the shoreline of Point Reyes in the late April pre-dawn hours, muffling the sounds of the waves pounding the shore. Tide was coming in.

A large harbor seal, sleek and spotted, bodysurfed right up to the sandy shore, and hauled itself out of the water onto the kelp-covered sand, as ungainly on land as it was graceful in the water, caterpillar-inching its way above the water mark.

Two curious reddish brown Tule elk up on the ridgeline watched, nostrils flaring, as the seal shimmered, as its form blurred. They weren't alarmed. They'd seen this before.

A man holding a sealskin appeared in place of the seal. He shook his head like a dog shaking to dry his fur after a bath, water droplets spraying from his long grey and black streaked hair. The chill air didn't seem to bother him. His face was youthful despite the grey hair, with lean features and long-lashed, dark brown eyes. A jagged, faded, half circular scar, at least twelve inches across, marred his thickly muscled torso, a reminder of a shark attack when he was a juvenile, frolicking off the Farallons, well south of Point Reyes.

His stride as walked up the beach to the trailhead was loose and relaxed.

He knelt and dug in the sand by the trail sign, finally reaching the lid to a 10 gallon dog food bin he'd buried there, ever since he started his job as a ranger two years ago and knew he'd be going back and forth between the sea and land. He spun the lid open and retrieved a stuffed backpack and his wallet.

He dressed rapidly, pulling on loose-fitting, ripped up faded blue jeans and a UC Santa Cruz sweatshirt, forcing his damp sandy feet into worn dirty white sneakers. He rolled up the sealskin and tucked it into the empty backpack. He closed the lid to the bin, then covered it back up with the excavated sand.

He slung the backpack over his left shoulder, then began the hike to the Kenneth C. Patrick visitor center parking lot, where he'd left his car the night before.

The Tule elk froze, ears pricked. Then bolted.

A gunshot cracked against the rising sun.

The man spun and fell, dropping the backpack, blood rapidly staining his grey sweatshirt and the sand beneath him black.

JOLENE STUCK her nose as deep as she could into the brandy-snifter shaped glass, and inhaled. Bliss. Chocolate and coffee and booze and just a hint of smoked cherry wood. She tasted just a tiny bit, letting it roll over her tongue. Oooh, yes. Bourbon barrel aged imperial stout from 2014. Decadent with a capital D. This is why she loved this taproom. Over a hundred beers on tap. The best list, week after week, she'd ever come across. Never mind the sticky concrete floors, the rickety tables and stools, or the rank cotton candy and not so fresh fish odor wafting in from the marina. The beer topped everything.

"Whatcha think?" asked Steve, the bartender, leaning across the stained warped bartop. He had poured it without even asking what she'd like.

"Heaven, just heaven. Got any bottles?"

"Nah, just the one keg. And before you ask, no growlers. And yes, once it's gone, it's gone. I don't think any other taproom in the US has this anymore. So drink up."

"Thanks, Steve." She snagged the snifter and walked over to one of the tables by the open windows overlooking the boardwalk. She hopped up onto a stool.

Sea lions were barking, but other than that, it was a quiet weekday spring evening. Too early in the year for lots of tourists at the pier and boardwalk.

Sun was going to be setting in just a minute or two, and she could just see the horizon past the moored sailboats and fishing boats, past the artificial rock and concrete breakwater.

She wanted to catch the green flash.

Three, two, one...the sun set...wait for it...and her view was suddenly blocked by a tall, lanky, androgynous figure, clothed in a loose faded blue t-shirt and dark jeans. Long dark hair streamed damply over their shoulders, and their eyes glowed like backlit amber.

"I require your assistance again," they said, their voice like sand being blown across a tarp.

So much for enjoying her beer.

Last time she'd seen them, they'd scared the beejesus out of her, revealing themself in all their sea god or goddess splendor (aka something out of the eldritch terrors), before haring off to slaughter her previous client in, admittedly, well deserved revenge.

Jolene was a private investigator with a few special talents: the ability to talk to the little creatures like rats and pigeons, and more importantly, the ability to use the Sense, to mentally step down or sideways and see, hear, taste, or smell magic and the otherworld. That meant that her clients were often on the unusual side.

Like Ursula-Trident standing there.

Who kinda looked a little like a prettier, really young, late 1960s Iggy Pop at this point. All big eyes and long lashes and cheek bones and that super lean physique.

"Folks in hell want a sip of iced water," she said. She closed her eyes. *Sideways.* Opened. The lanky figure was taller, thinner, creepier, cloaked in a seaweed-dripping robe, and their eyes shone Garibaldi orange. Their face glittered in the lights from behind the bar, tiny scales reflecting pale rainbows.

But, overall, nonthreatening.

She closed her eyes. *Back.* Reopened. Young Iggy still stood there patiently. She sighed.

"Okay, come in. We can talk. No promises though."

They nodded, then entered the bar, stopping at the counter first, where Steve already had a beer poured for them. Jolene raised an eyebrow. The two chitchatted briefly, Steve tossing his head back with a guffaw, then Iggy came over, dragging a second stool to her table, carefully placing their beer on the table.

"What'd he pick for you?" she asked.

"El Segundo Power Plant," they said in satisfaction. She nodded. It was good, a piney, grapefruity local triple IPA that managed to be balanced despite all the hops and high alcohol content.

"So, what should I call you?" she asked. Not asking for their name; that could be at best rude, at worst a deadly mistake. But she wanted to be polite.

They stared at her, then cocked their head. "Iggy will do."

Oops. But already they — he? — began looking more masculine, delicate features thickening a tiny bit, shoulders broadening, arms more muscled.

"One of mine was murdered two nights ago," Iggy said. "North, north of San Francisco. A selkie who was employed as a ranger at Point Reyes National Seashore. I would like you to find out who did it."

"Aren't the local police working on it?"

Iggy shrugged. "They can't *see*, like you. They won't have all the information they need."

Jolene drummed her fingers on the tabletop, took a big sip of her beer. "I just don't know —" She had several small jobs in progress, but truly nothing urgent. Nothing like a life lost.

"They took his sealskin, Jolene. Whoever did it knew what he was." Pain flooded Iggy's eyes. "I cannot force you to help. However: please. As a favor to me and mine."

She stared at him, at those alien amber eyes, then nodded. "I'll do it. But it's not cheap—"

Iggy waved his hand. "No matter. I have dear friend, a human friend, who I can put you in contact with in the town of Point Reyes Station. She has a guest house she rents out, where you can stay. She will help you work with the police." He paused, then, softly, "Can you leave tonight?"

"First thing in the morning," said Jolene. "Before dawn."

Iggy had handed her a stack of bills, more than enough for her retainer, expenses, and a week's worth of work, as well as the address and phone number for his friend Doria Masters. She was glad he'd not presented a water-soaked bag of doubloons, though she wouldn't have been surprised. Despite his facility for passing as human, he seemed old fashioned, courtly.

She left Redondo Beach by 4:30 a.m. and was well along the 5, Interstate 5, chugging along in her old Chevy Nova, long before any hint of rush hour traffic, letting an Americano with two extra shots of espresso and the rapid picking of Dick Dale wake her up. She was streaming music from her phone to a blue tooth speaker, so the sound quality wasn't the greatest, but the fast paced surf music always energized her.

By 3 p.m. she was pulling through a wisteria-draped white painted wooden archway into Doria's driveway, gravel crunching under her tires. The sweet musky scent of the wisteria, touched by brine from nearby Tomales Bay, flooded in as she rolled down her window.

A pretty charcoal grey gabled and yellow shingled cottage, with a wraparound porch that reminded her of her granny's farmhouse in East Texas, sat at the end of the driveway. A white-haired, trim woman wearing a straw hat, t-shirt, and khaki pants was methodically gathering a bouquet, pink and peach and yellow tea roses intermingled with long stems of lavender, from a front yard that seemed to consist entirely of flowers and herbs and curved pea gravel paths. The woman looked up and waved.

"Park at the end of the driveway," the woman called, her voice surprisingly husky and strong.

Sacrificed bodies in the cellar. Something. There had to be something to make up for all this country perfection.

"I'm Doria Masters. Care for a glass of mead after that long drive? There's a local meadery just north of town," she continued as Jolene parked and got out. "They're a bit uppity, but the mead is wonderful."

Yep, bodies somewhere.

"That would be very nice," Jolene said. "Thank you kindly."

"Maris is greatly impressed by you," she said, her voice flat. "I hope you can help. She had only kind words about you."

Maris? Oh, Iggy. Interesting. She'd seen a display on clownfish at the aquarium in Long Beach that talked about them changing gender. Guess that applied to, well, whatever Iggy was.

Doria brushed Jolene aside, hauling Jolene's fully packed Army green canvas duffel bag out of the back seat, brushing aside Jolene's attempts to grab it. "Guesthouse first."

The guesthouse was cute as a button, with aqua painted clapboard sides, a tin roof, and a tiny porch with room enough just for a rope hammock with some pillows. Immediately inside was a double bed with a faded flower garden patterned quilt (upon which Doria tossed the duffel bag), tucked up between the doorway and the leftmost wall. A desk with a vase of cut lavender was tucked in the nook against the far wall. A bureau set up with a microwave and a coffee machine on top of it, and a dorm sized refrigerator lined up along the window-filled wall opposite the bed.

An enclosed small bath, barely big enough for the toilet, cast iron tub, and pedestal sink, took up the far corner of the room.

A leather 3-ring binder sat on the wooden desk.

"Info on WiFi, local restaurants, etc," Doria told her, hefting the binder then replacing it. "I'll cook you breakfast each morning if you'd like."

"That would be lovely," Jolene said.

"But let's get down to business, right? Meet me on the front porch."

~

TWENTY MINUTES LATER, face freshly washed and feeling a bit more human, Jolene sat at the bistro table on Doria's front deck, sipping the last bit of a crisp, floral mead and flipping through what looked to be a copy of an official police report.

"My son James is a detective in the local sheriff's department," Doria said, her tanned, lined face haggard close up. "Patrick, the selkie, was my godson."

"One round," Jolene said. It had caused terrible damage, shredding lung tissue, obliterating Patrick's heart, and splintering ribs, according to the coroner's report. She looked at the crime scene photo, Patrick's sprawled body, his bloody sweatshirt. She squinted, but she couldn't *see* anything about the photo, no otherworldly impressions.

Frankly, she didn't expect to. The Sense worked in real time, in real space, not through pictures or drawings.

"James doesn't know what Patrick was," Doria continued. "He just knew him as the son of my friend Estella. They grew up like brothers."

"The coroner didn't find anything unusual?"

"Selkies look completely human without their sealskin. I suppose if Dr Jay had done any sort of toxicology screens, or any other sort of lab work, maybe things would look odd, especially with Paddy dead and any glamour wearing off."

"Quick turnaround on the coroner's side."

"He's also a GP practicing in Santa Rosa, volunteers with the coroner's office as needed. It's really quiet here, usually."

"Well, from this, it looks like the shooter knew what he was doing and had planned in advance. He knew where to find Patrick, what to steal."

"Estella needs that sealskin back," Doria said. "For it to be missing, for someone to be misusing it, it's tearing her apart. That's why Maris sent you."

"And the sheriff's department concluded it was random killing?"

"And the FBI. Federal land. They have no idea about the skin. As far as they know, Patrick was on an early morning hike and just came across his murderer. Wrong place, wrong time.

"He was quiet, but friendly, no enemies. Kept to himself. Visited his family in the ocean more often than not, more nights out there than at his apartment. Sometimes he'd ruffle the feathers of a few of the tourists who didn't follow park rules, but other than that..."

"I know it's getting late, but can someone show me where he died? I think I need to look, really *look*."

"Maris told me what you can do. I can take you out there." She eyed Jolene's jeans and t-shirt. "Bring a jacket. It gets cold quick."

THEY REACHED the shore right before sunset. The last of the sun's rays set the cirrus clouds ablaze with vivid oranges and pinks, that faded to grey violet as they both exited Jolene's Chevy.

The touch of sea spray bouncing off the rocks below tasted like sharp briny little icicles. Jolene huddled into her sweatshirt, pulling the hood up over her head. She was glad she was wearing jeans and hiking shoes. This wasn't her ocean back home in Los Angeles. The water was cold there too, but not like this. Not as icy. Not as wild.

"The light house is that way," Doria pointed west. "But Paddy was shot down closer to Drakes Beach, by the estuary." She pointed back north-northeast. "I thought you could get a good feel for the terrain from up here."

Point Reyes was a peninsula, with the lighthouse atop the cliffs at the west-most edge. Drakes Bay curved east, heading north a bit then diving back south. Tomales Bay, actually the last terrestrial bit of the San Andreas Fault, split the peninsula from the bulk of the mainland.

It wasn't that many square miles, but there was a wildness to the waves and forests and cliffs, even to the smooth sandy beaches along the curve of Drake's Bay, especially in early evening with no one else around.

"Seen enough up here," Jolene said.

They drove silently to the visitor center by Drakes Beach. When Jolene parked, Doria refused to get out.

"I just can't," Doria said. "The trail is marked, you can find it." Grief tightened her features.

Jolene didn't argue, just reached past Doria to grab a flashlight from the glove compartment. The spring twilight was lingering, and she could feel the moon rising, but better safe than sorry. Last thing she needed was to run into a branch of poison oak.

The hike down to the beach was pleasant. Jolene could hear the rustlings of small mammals and other creatures as she walked. She didn't know if any would deign to talk to her. She hoped they would, that they were inured to the presence of humans. Shoot, if she'd planned better she'd've brought some snacks for the ground squirrels. Rats with good PR, she'd never seen a ground squirrel in a touristy area that turned down popcorn or cheese doodles.

Seagulls squawked overhead, flying to settle in for the evening. One of those might do, if she couldn't find a talkative ground squirrel.

She stepped over police tape stretched across the path and paused by the trailhead marker. The bloody sand had been removed, or rinsed, or something, because it all looked and smelled normal. Just sand and ocean air and a sharp floral scent, bay laurel trees and coyote bushes.

Doria had mentioned that Patrick had buried a bin to keep clothes in, for when he left the sea and came back to land, by the trailhead, and that it was still there, buried. No reason it pull it up.

Of course, officials wouldn't have known it was there. Just Doria, and whoever killed Patrick.

Enough nattering. She closed her eyes, breathed deeply. She hated this part. She would be vulnerable, and she hated that.

Down.

She didn't have to go far, feeling the shift from her normal reality to the otherworld like a nudge against her belly. Wild indeed. She opened her eyes.

The clouds here retained some of that sunset fire, violet touched flames flickering along the edges of the feathery wisps of cirrus.

Stars glittered towards the east. Glowing aquamarine phosphorescence tipped the crests of the waves and coloured the seafoam that lingered on the beach. Rich saltiness, like fresh oysters, tickled her tongue.

And the shimmering grey image of the most beautiful man she'd ever seen flickered in front of her, then spun and hit the ground, over and over again. Shock and pain and betrayal, over and over again.

Too much. Too close. She felt that vicious punch of the bullet in her chest, took his last ragged gasp for air herself. Over and over again.

She fainted.

~

It was full dark when she came to, tickled by the dampness of a tiny tongue lapping against her cheek. She was back in her world, the jewel-like stars and ocean fire banked behind reality.

The moon had fully risen, a soft bulbous yellow globe, and gave her enough light to see the little ground squirrel by her face, poised to lick again, its beady black eyes meeting hers.

Yep, pretty tame. Cute little thing.

Selkie? she thought at it.

It went rigid, then fled. All she could feel from it was violent death. That she knew already. No other trace of anything otherworldly besides Patrick and his sealskin.

She didn't know what that meant, that repeating ghostly image. She'd never seen that before, but suspected it was because his sealskin was stolen. Likely Estella's son couldn't rest until it was found.

Times like now she wished she had a Faerie hound, a beast that could track on both sides. She didn't have the nose or the skill to track the skin herself.

She ached all over. A psychic punching bag. She hauled herself up, dusting off sand. She walked stiffly back to the car.

Doria was taking a nap, head back at an awkward angle. Even through the rolled-up windows Jolene could hear a soft snore. Jolene suspected she'd been passed out from the wallop from Patrick's death for more than an hour. Couldn't blame Doria for getting a bit of rest.

She tapped gently on the driver's side window, trying to wake Doria up without scaring the bejeesus out of her.

Sorta worked. Jolene gingerly lowered herself into the driver's seat, started up the car, and said, "Not much luck. Think I could talk to James tonight, if it's not too late?" She didn't want to tell Doria about Patrick's ghost. Too hurtful, no point.

"Let me call him," Doria said, voice still thick with sleep.

Doria navigated the narrow winding road carefully, watching for deer, as Doria chatted with James.

"We can meet him for a late supper," Doria said, hanging up on James. "He's got a place in Petaluma."

THEY PULLED UP TO JAMES' apartment building at 9:05 pm. Jolene's stomach had been growling and grumbling for the last half hour. She didn't like missing meals. Using the Sense yanked energy out of her like a piglet taking his second suckle.

The apartment complex looked like a refurbished 1970s two-story motel, with a balcony that stretched across the second floor entrances and a small pale swimming pool, caged in wrought iron fencing, taking up half the parking lot. Builder beige paint, flaking a bit, on the siding, dark brown doors and window trim. Bland. Nicest thing was the scent of jasmine that rolled over her as they got out of the car and headed up the concrete and steel staircase to the second floor.

At the top of the stairs, Doria placed her hand on Jolene's arm. "He's sick," she said. "He insisted on getting involved on the case, and the sheriff let him. Don't say anything about his health. Treat him normal."

James' apartment was an end unit, at the far end from the staircase. Jolene could smell garlic and onions and meat as they approached, and she couldn't help her mouth watering.

"Come on in. Door's open." The male version of Doria's husky voice, but underlaid with weariness.

The apartment was nicer on the inside than she would have expected from the dull outside. Dark greyish-brown plank laminate floors, a retro-style saddle tan leather sofa, red and pink and cream vintage wool Persian rugs. As an end unit, it sported windows along the front and the side, all draped with mossy brown floor length velvet curtains that contrasted with the cream painted walls. It looked like a minimalist gentleman's smoking club. Without any tobacco odor.

It had an open floor plan, so she could see James in the kitchen, draining a big pot of rigatoni into a colander, his bony wrists trembling with the weight of the pot. "Mom, can you get the garlic toast out of the oven? And there's a salad in the fridge."

The butcher-block topped island was already set with bowls, plates, napkins and silverware. A small bowl of nutty, freshly grated parmesan caught her attention. She loved cheese.

"If I know my mom, all she gave you was some of that darn mead," he said to Jolene. "I'm sure you're starving by now." He smiled at her.

If Doria hadn't warned her, Jolene wouldn't have kept her client face on. James was tall, about six feet two to Jolene's five foot six, but she would be surprised if he even topped her muscular 150 lbs. He was rail thin, his cheekbones and wrists sharp, and he had a paleness that eclipsed that of Paddy's ghost. His short, dark brown hair was dull and brittle and streaked with grey.

But his dark indigo blue eyes were soft and his smile sweet, and Jolene instinctively liked him.

He dished out generous heaps of pasta into each bowl, topping it with garlicky, rich meat sauce. "Sit. Eat. Then we can talk."

The pasta sauce had a rich, meaty, almost gamy taste, and Jolene cleaned her plate and devoured seconds as well, wiping up the last bits of sauce with the crunchy garlic toast. Doria picked at her meal.

"Like it?" James asked Jolene. "Costco organic beef mixed with some ground up wild pig that Mom caught last fall. I'm not keen on hunting, but the boars are a nuisance, destroying native habitat."

"Delicious," Jolene said. "Bay leaves, thyme... nutmeg?"

"Good palate. And a little cinnamon," he said. "Weird but it works." He picked up their bowls and plates and stacked them in the sink.

"So. I don't know if Mom told you, but I'm on medical leave from the department. Sheriff Garcia shared the file with me as a favor." Grief ghosted his eyes, darkening them to black. "Mom said you might be able to help, so I'm grasping at straws."

"I'm not sure that I can help," Jolene said. "But I'm willing to try." She avoided looking at Doria.

"Thanks," he said.

"I think, though, that I need to go back to the beach. Just to check something." She paused. "I don't mean to be rude, but—"

"A really rare type of non-Hodgkins lymphoma," James said. "Non-responsive to chemo so far. It's okay. I have one last round of chemo to try."

"I'm really sorry," Jolene said.

He shrugged, smiled that sweet smile. "Thanks."

~

JOLENE CAREFULLY BACKED the Chevy out of the parking space, knuckles whitened.

"He looks like Patrick," she said quietly. "A stretched-out version."

"Some Selkie blood, generations back, on his dad's side," Doria said. "Estella told me."

"Boar hunting, huh?" She had almost insisted that she drive back alone, racing through the softly rolling hills back to Point Reyes Station, to that little farmhouse, to rip it apart searching for the sealskin before Doria could find her way back.

Bodies in the cellar indeed.

But she wasn't sure if the sealskin was there, and she was pretty sure she could take a sixty year old woman, no matter how tough and determined, in a hand to hand fight.

Not sure if she'd go up against Doria at a shooting range, though.

Stoplight. Red. Jolene glanced *sideways* at Doria.

Blood coated Doria's hands and arms like shiny red latex.

"You know," Jolene said, looking at the red glow of the stoplight back in the real world, "when I was just a kid, I didn't know how to control the Sense. My teachers would find me in the playground, standing stock still, drool dripping off my chin, the other kids mocking and laughing, as I stared at the otherworld, fascinated by the pretty lights and colours. My granny pulled me out of school, home-schooled me, including teaching me how to control the Sense; to use it, not let it use me."

Doria fidgeted.

"So I *don't* use it, hardly at all, unless there's a specific need. So I didn't look at you, with your hands dripping blood."

"I—" the older woman trailed off.

"And maybe I trust too much. Because I do think you loved Patrick. Just you love your son more," Jolene continued. "Do you really think the sealskin will cure him?"

"*They* don't get sick. *They* don't die of old age," Doria said, her voice ragged. "I don't know, but I had to try."

"This is between you and Estella. And Maris," Jolene said, glancing at Doria. "The FBI or the sheriff's department, they don't have priority on this. Not to me."

They drove in silence the rest of the way to Doria's farmhouse. Jolene thought about letting Doria out at the wisteria-covered archway and just driving away, but she wanted her duffel bag, sitting on that faded flower garden quilt on the guestroom bed.

She'd left her computer in that bag, let alone her favorite handknit sweater. Not sure if her bag was enough to risk getting shot, but darn it, she didn't give up.

Jolene backed into the driveway, gravel crunching, slamming the brakes as an owl swept by in her rear view mirror.

"Stay here," Jolene said. She got out, projected in the direction the owl had flown. *Favor?*

The owl flew back to her out of the darkness and perched on the roof of the car, rocking back and forth in surprise. It was a barn owl, with a broad cream-feathered face and a pretty speckled chest.

Guard? Jolene asked. The barn owl settled in, stopped rocking.

She ran to the guesthouse and grabbed her duffel before she heard an awful racket of screeching and screaming.

Sure enough, Doria had left the car. The owl fluttered back down onto the car roof, agitated, blood on its face and beak, but Doria was nowhere to be seen.

Time to git. She could just picture Doria grabbing a hunting rifle and coming after her. Didn't need the Sense to see that. Doria was stuck between a gator and quicksand and they both knew it.

Jolene tossed her bag across the driver's seat to the passenger seat and followed it in, getting the key in the ignition and her foot on the accelerator before she even shut the door.

She saw Doria in her rear view mirror, tearing out the house, rifle in hand, then pausing to carefully aim.

Jolene floored the accelerator, thinking of that perfect moonlit shot that splintered Patrick's heart.

A bullet struck the edge of the back window, causing the window itself to shatter. The scents of gunpowder and wisteria flooded the car.

The owl divebombed Doria, talons reaching for her face.

Jolene was back on the main road before Doria could get off a second shot, bless her heart.

~

JOLENE DROVE TO DRAKES BEACH. She wasn't sure how to contact Estella, but had a grisly hope that she might be near the place of her son's death. Worth a try, anyhow.

Tide was out, and the beach smelled of kelp and salty tears. Jolene took off her sneakers, rolled up her jeans, and waded just ankle deep, letting the icy Pacific taste her skin. *Down.*

That turquoise phosphorescence lit up the sand and water around her cold feet. Pretty, so pretty. The moon, near to setting, glowed a soft white and smiled down at her.

She didn't dare look at the trailhead.

"Estella," she called. "Estella, Estella."

She smelled flowers salted with brine, and the head of a female harbor seal, sleek and spotted, popped up from the gentle waves. The seal barked, then swam in to shore, hauling herself up onto the beach. She shimmered, and Jolene couldn't quite see the transformation, just hints of sealskin and human flesh, til a woman, just under her own height, with voluptuous curves, an ageless face, and dark hair streaming down her back, stood before Jolene.

"The hound of the Sea," Estella said. "Thank you."

Jolene didn't know what *that* meant. Or at least didn't care for the implications. Hound? She would worry about it later when she saw Iggy again.

"I know who killed your son," Jolene said, and told her the whole sorry story.

When she had finished, Estella took her hands. "Thank you, again." Rage and grief and betrayal filled her eyes, so similar to what had played across her son Patrick's face in that ghostly replay.

They both heard the car pull up.

Clouds scudded across the face of the moon, darkening their portion of the beach, hiding them. The trailhead was lit up like a spotlight, though.

"I know you're here!" called Doria. Her cheeks bore blood-streaked talon marks.

Superimposed, invisible to Doria but clearly seen by Jolene, was the ghostly form of Patrick. He wasn't reliving his death this time; rather, he stood still, staring at Doria, face tight.

"Jolene, show yourself!"

They both heard the click of the safety.

Estella raised a finger to her lips. "Stay here," she whispered. Jolene nodded.

She turned, then stepped *sideways*. Jolene could see two images of Estella, both walking towards the trailhead, towards Doria: one naked, gait loose and easy, one clothed in faded jeans and a dark coloured sweater.

"Too late, Doria," Estella said. "Jolene told me what you did."

"Estella?"

"Where is my son's sealskin?" Both images reached out.

Doria hunched back, for the first time looking all of her sixty plus years. "I'm so sorry, Estella." She straightened, raised the rifle to her shoulder, and fired.

At the woman wearing jeans and a sweater. Who dissipated into moon-kissed fog.

The naked woman swung a sharp-clawed hand at Doria's throat, ripping through the front of her neck.

Patrick's ghost straightened, spun with the force of *his* gunshot wound, hit the ground, and bled, moonlit blood black, soaking the sand.

Doria collapsed, blood soaking the same sand as Patrick's.

Patrick's form faded away when she stopped breathing.

JOLENE DROVE BACK to Doria's farmhouse, the cold night air whistling in through her empty back windshield sharpening her focus on the dark curves of the two lane road. Estella had assured her that Doria's body would disappear —"It's an honor to feed the sea, and once, she was my friend"—and had given Jolene explicit instructions to pass on to James, on her way back to Los Angeles.

But first, Jolene needed to find the sealskin, shower, and sleep.

The sealskin wasn't even hidden. It lay upon a twin bed, in a small bedroom filled with trophies and sports posters, that she assumed had been James', growing up. The sealskin was soft and warm and supple, spotted cream and charcoal, and when she looked, just a little *sideways*, she could see it softly glowing, the tips of the short fur glistening.

That glow brightened when she handed it to James, the next morning. He glowed, too, when she *looked*, barely more than human, but there it was. She wasn't sure if he believed her, when she told him to skip chemo and go to the ocean, find a quiet private spot, and wrap the sealskin around his butt-naked body.

She told him to go to Drakes Beach and call for Estella if he didn't believe her.

Estella could tell him about his mama, and what she did. Jolene didn't have the heart to do it.

If she was a hound, she was a *hound*. Not a tell-tale.

But she did leave him her number, and instructions to call afterwards.

He had a sweet smile.

THE LITTLE ANIMALS, THE VERMIN, OF VENICE

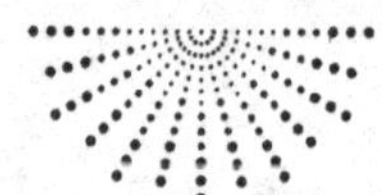

*D*otty sipped bitter espresso from the tiny chipped porcelain cup, inhaling the rich scent, gazing out kitty-corner over the Piazza at St Mark's Cathedral from Café Florian. She crossed her liquid-stockinged, goose-pimpled legs at her slim ankles.

Her dove gray wool jacket and skirt set was Italian, from Milano, and five years out of date, but it was appropriate for a young woman suffering from the hardships of war. It did little to keep her warm on this chilly overcast March morning, but it wouldn't catch anyone's attention.

Unfortunately, her golden blonde hair, delphinium blue eyes, and fine features *did* garner her more attention than she wanted: catcalls, murmured invitations, ragged men dogging her footsteps.

Annoying, but she could deal with all that. A sharp *Basta*!, a pointy heel jammed onto a foot.

More importantly, the denizens of Venice, male and female, assumed her Northern Italian, maybe from the Lake Country near Switzerland, waiting out the war in one of the safer locales in Italy. (No one, Allies or Axis, wanted to bomb Venice, a world treasure of history and architecture and art.)

She looked Northern Italian, or maybe even Swiss.

Not an American spy.

She tossed some breadcrumbs onto the paving stones. A flock of pigeons rushed in, shoving each other for the precious morsels. Little rats of the sky. Dotty smiled fondly.

Dotty crumbled more breadcrumbs from the crust of her small baguette, coaxing a particularly fine, plump pigeon closer. His bright amber eyes met hers with a simple avian greediness, and he puffed his splendid pale gray feathered chest as he strutted closer.

He looked healthy enough he could fly far. At least the 80 or so odd miles to Cervia, as the pigeon flies.

He would do.

She held out her hand. *Talk? Palare?* she projected.

If a pigeon could look shocked, this one did, chest deflating and wings tensing for flight.

A small scrappy female shoved him out of the way. *Mollica*, she demanded. *Crumb*. She hopped up onto Dotty's hand, helping herself to the baguette, one red eye locked onto Dotty's face while she ate.

Ships. Dotty projected her earlier-morning view of the Venetian harbor, filled with German transport, escort and cargo ships, as well as an *Ariete* class torpedo ship. *Guns*. The guns along the docks.

Navi, agreed the pigeon. She projected the image back to Dotty, clear as the pigeon had seen it herself. Who said pigeons were dumb?

Dotty kept feeding the little pigeon crumbs. Fifteen more minutes til the clock tower rang noon, when her younger sister Frankie would *project*, to serve as a homing beacon for the pigeon, with Dotty the link between the two. Dotty didn't have that kind of strength or range, which was why she was here in Venice, and Frankie was back at the Cervia airbase, waiting with the No. 250 RAF squadron.

Ten minutes. Five. She finished her espresso, wishing there had been even a tiny bit of sugar to sweeten it. No luck there, not with rationing.

The sun finally broke through the clouds, patches of bright blue sky appearing above head.

The bell starting ringing, echoed by church bells through the city, the sounds racing along the canals. Dotty stroked the pigeon's sleek back. *Ready, little one?*

Dong. Dong. Dong.

A form blotted out the sunlight.

"Fraulein?" A German Naval officer, thin in his midnight blue uniform, stood before her. "Fraulein, you must come with me. Now." English.

She ignored him. *Frankie*, she pleaded. *NOW!* She knew Frankie couldn't hear her, even if Dotty had had her sister's reach: Dotty was only able to speak to the little ones, the vermin, rats and pigeons and squirrels and sparrows, maybe a rabbit on a good day.

Dong. Dong. Dong.

" Fraulein, devi venire con me. Adesso!" He swatted at the little pigeon, knocking her off Dotty's hand.

The pigeon fell limply to the paving stones. The officer had broken her neck. Both Dotty and the officer stared down at the pigeon in shock.

The rest of the pigeons had retreated, pacing nervously, fluttering up and down. Dotty scanned them, found the big male, met his fearful amber eyes. *SHIPS! GUNS!*

The male started seizing. Too much! She sagged, sick with guilt, as he continued to seize. Then his violent twitching stopped, and he didn't move at all.

She didn't even notice the officer grasping her arm, dragging her to her feet.

Dong. Dong. Dong.

She hadn't any sort of bond with any of the other pigeons.

She had failed.

The last bell peal rang across the Piazza. The pigeons scattered.

FRANKIE HUDDLED at the worn wooden desk, head down, dark hair streaming across her face, clutching a pencil so hard she broke it. She looked up, out the small window to the airfield full of Kittyhawks and

Mustangs. The clock above the window snicked to 12:01 p.m., the sound harsh in the tiny office.

"No response," Frankie said, pushing her long dark hair out of her face, not waiting for the surrounding RAF officers to ask. She'd gotten nothing at nine, or ten, or eleven, but she had fully expected to reach her sister at noon.

The airstrike was scheduled for two days away, pending confirmation of targets.

Oh, they hadn't told her that, but the thought was easy enough for her to pick off the top of their minds. She didn't tell them she could do that. Dotty was limited to the smaller creatures. Frankie wasn't. Far as she was concerned, that was her business. An ace in the hole.

She wasn't as pretty or elegant as Dotty, with narrow dark features and a sturdy build, but she was a good site better when it came to their gifts. She chafed that Dotty got to have all the adventure —*Venezia*! the city of canals, and merchants, and history—and she was stuck with a passel of fighter pilots, safe in the rear. Didn't help that she was working inside a stuffy, sweaty smelling office, just sitting. Didn't matter that some of those pilots were prettier than a speckled pup, and nearly all longing for female companionship. She couldn't care a fig for that.

She wanted adventure, darn it. That's why she became a spy.

Though Lieutenant Joseph Hirsch seemed to appreciate her for her gifts. And he did have those warm hazel eyes, that curly dark hair that looked so soft.

"There's a recon flight heading out later," he noted. "Worst case, we'll get the intel that way."

"Doesn't help," she said. "That will be from 10,000 feet up, not 60 feet up on a building by the harbor. You wanted details. That's why we're here."

Some of the men shifted uneasily. Frankie didn't care. Bunch of scaredy-cats outside their planes. A'scared of a witchy girl like her or her sister. "I'll try again, on the hour, til 6 pm." *And if I don't reach Dotty by then, I'm getting myself to Venice, tonight.*

~

Dotty sat limply on a hard, wooden chair, hands tied snugly behind her, wrists aching, chafed from the rough rope. A single uncovered light bulb hung over her head, a spotlight of illumination. Not that she could see much, harsh yellow light or not, with both eyes swollen half-shut.

She was alone. Finally. The room was dank, water from the canals seeping through the walls, and smelled of mold and old blood and rat piss. The floor was rough stone pavers, the walls exposed brick. She suspected this room, a flight of stairs down from the main floor, was under the current water level of the canals.

The young Naval captain was long gone. The flash of pity in his eyes, as he turned her over to the Gestapo agent, didn't mean squat to her.

"We know you are an American spy," the Gestapo agent had told her, what seemed like hours ago. He accented each word with an open-handed slap. He wasn't as tall as the naval officer, but was bulkier. Thuggish, with heavy, ruddy features and long-lashed light blue eyes that had all the emotion of a china doll's. He wore civilian clothes, a loose-fitting dark gray suit, a worn white collared shirt, and thin black leather gloves.

"You think this pretty face will save you?" A fist to her left eye, cutting her eyelid.

She sat mute. Even if she wanted to talk, she knew he wouldn't believe her. Leastwise not about talking to pigeons. She smirked, earning a punch that split her lip.

What was her mission?

Who were her contacts?

What information had she already passed on?

A hundred different versions, all the same questions. She said nothing, just sobbed when it hurt so much she couldn't *not* cry. She had no idea of how long the interrogation had lasted. She couldn't hear anything from outside the room, not even the church bells.

She felt a soft wet nose at her fingertips, a tentative nuzzle, and she straightened, whimpering from the pain of moving even that much.

" I will leave you to the rats, if you don't talk," the agent said, his thuggish features tightening in disgust, though his tone was even.

"Leave me, then," she whispered. Her blood coating his gloves was fine, but a rat made him squeamish?

"As you will," he said. "You'll be screaming for me to come back, soon enough."

He'd left, leaving the light on. She assumed he thought the sight of the rats creeping towards her would break her. Joke's on him. Gestapo bastard.

Rope? she asked. Several squeaks of affirmation, and she could feel tiny spurts of warm breath near her wrists. They must be stretching to try to reach the ropes. She rocked the chair til she fell sideways.

Once the ropes were within their reach, the gnawing went quickly. She'd seen rats chew through bricks. Rope, however thick, was nothing to their sharp sturdy incisors.

Thank you. Still laying on her side, she massaged her wrists, wincing as her hands prickled. Soon enough the pain would be downright miserable, possibly debilitating. She already ached all over. Blows to her face had alternated with vicious punches to her gut. She figured she'd be pissing blood. She rolled to her knees, then stood up, slowly, slowly, biting her lip to keep from crying out. She staggered to the heavy wooden door, tripping over her jacket, yanked off of her and tossed onto the floor before she was restrained on the chair. She picked it up, shrugged it on gingerly, buttoned it. It covered her blood-soaked silk blouse, at least, and would keep her a tiny bit warm, assuming she got out of the villa.

She tried the heavy iron knob, exhaling as she did so.

It turned.

It was unlocked.

Thank the good lord above for men who underestimated a woman's cunning.

She opened the door, just a crack, cringing as the hinges creaked, the sound echoing down the dimly lit hallway beyond. One, two, three rats squeezed through. *Recon*, she projected. Two dashed to the left, towards the staircase, from where she'd been dragged to this room, and one towards the right. That one came back immediately. Nothing but more rooms with shut doors and another staircase, with water lapping at the mossy stone steps, at the very end of the hallway.

She counted the seconds, the minutes, til the one of the other two returned. He sat up, meeting her eyes, twitching his whiskers.

? she thought at him, then nodded in thanks at his response. No one at the stairs, but the rats couldn't hear anything, or smell anything, beyond the heavy oak door, twin to the one next to her, at the top. The other rat waited there, ready to let them know if anyone was approaching. She had to take the chance; she couldn't stay down here.

She slipped out the door, then crept up the stairs, heart pounding so hard she was sure if there was a guard, they would hear it, despite the thick wooden door at the top. The door was firmly shut. She didn't dare try the doorknob willy-nilly. She pressed her ear against the door, but heard nothing beyond it.

She had to just do it.

But first ... she *called*, asking, pleading, begging for help. And the rats came, more and more rats, til the stairs and the landing upon which she stood were carpeted by warm furry bodies, squeaking and skittering.

She grasped the knob, turned it. Now or never.

～

No response to Frankie's on-the-hour projections, bolstered by her increasing worry, winging outwards into nothingness. She barely nibbled on a late lunch, a bit of canned meat and a piece of coarse unsalted bread, chased by watered wine, though her abilities cost her energy-wise, and she needed to eat to sustain her efforts.

In between projections, unable to rest and unable to concentrate, she tried to review maps to Venice.

Six p.m., and that was it. She couldn't wait any longer.

And then came the news: the surveillance plane had been shot down in a fiery ball as it flew back from Venice.

All of a sudden, Dotty and Frankie's mission became critical. The squadron needed to know what the Germans had anchored in the Venetian harbor, to best choose when to risk, when to commit to, a bombing run. They would only have one chance. The Allies had taken over all other routes of supply from Italy; conclusively destroying this one would further cripple the German forces. Dotty had that information about the harbor, Frankie knew it; she didn't doubt her poised, focused older sister would succeed in that. But something had happened, must have happened, to keep her from passing it on.

"I need a car and a driver," Frankie told Westlake, the young handsome Wing Commander, balling her fists at her sides, straightening to her full five foot two.

"Can't do, Miss," he said. "I can send a couple men in, to look for her, but I can't send you. No use you finding her then not being able to get back here, for instance."

"I'll go," said Lieutenant Hirsch. His warm hazel eyes met Frankie's. "I'll find your sister."

Frankie could *feel* it, just off the top of his head, his worry for Dotty, tinged with desire, and his fondness for herself. Like for his scrappy kid sister, back in Whitechapel.

She sighed. Dotty, always Dotty. She guessed she couldn't blame Hirsch.

"Take two crewmen with you," Westlake said. "We need you back in one piece to fly."

"Yes, sir," Hirsch said, leaving the room.

"Miss Tomberlin, please keep checking for news of your sister," Westlake said, taking his leave as well.

She was alone. Darned if she was going to let Hirsch hightail it to Venice without her. She could be sneaky. She *excelled* at sneakiness.

So she snuck herself right under a tarp in the bed of the open cab deuce and half truck Lieutenant Hirsch had commandeered, while he was going through the last checkpoint out of the base. Just a little bit of mind-fogging of the nearby soldiers so they didn't catch a peek of her.

~

To Dotty's surprise and relief, no guard had been posted on the other side of the doorway, which was apparently just off the kitchen. She could hear pots clanking, running water, the steps of one person, maybe two, through the slightly ajar oak kitchen door. The smell of fresh bread, just baked, permeated the hallway.

She sent her rat army forward, dispersed along the hallway, dodging under and around the pieces of furniture, bureaus and chests and armoires, lining the walls, and into the different rooms of the main level. Sitting room, study, even a music room with an old grand piano. The cream, brown, and black terrazzo floors were carpeted with faded wool Persian rugs, muffling the sound of the rat's little claws. The cream colored plastered walls glowed softly in the yellow electrical lights. Whitewashed wooden beams extended across the ceiling. The mustiness of the basement was absent.

It was a fine palazzetto, unfortunately co-opted by the enemy, and would need extensive psychic cleansing by folks like her aunties after the war to be livable again for decent people.

One rat scampered back, squeaking excitedly. A bowl of stew, with a bit of beef and carrots and tomatoes, thyme and oregano. The dining room.

And the Gestapo agent, eating heartily. Not a care in the world, apparently, and no thought that the female American spy would have any chance of escape.

She could sneak out. She could. The rats showed her the route, a straight shot to the entry way, the heavy oak and iron doors that led out onto a landing, connected by a walkway to a passageway to the warren of smaller canals and buildings. From there she could get lost in the evening fog, maybe find a nightingale to get her information to Frankie.

She thought of the agent, his pleasure at beating her.

His aversion to the rats.

She shoved the nearest bureau across the kitchen door, hoping no one inside the kitchen would hear the scraping and creaking or her short gasps of pain as she exerted herself. The bureau, a lovely oak piece with inset ivory and ebony in a floral pattern across the drawers, must be stuffed with books. Or rocks.

She suspected there was a door from the kitchen directly to the dining room, but she couldn't do much about that. She straightened, wiped sweat and dust off her brow, then turned to the rats.

Mangiare, she thought to her army. *Eat.*

The screaming, shrill and panicked, had already turned to shrieks of maddened pain by the time she limped out of the palazzetto, into the quiet cool evening air.

THE DEUCE BRAKED SUDDENLY, tossing Frankie, still tucked under the tarp, against the front end of the bed. She figured they were halfway to Venice, from the time they'd been driving, rubbing her shoulder.

She didn't dare poke her head out to see what was going on.

Rather, she *sought*. And found an owl, ghosting across the road on pillow soft wings, above the generator-powered search lights on either side of a haphazard barricade across the road. *See?* she asked, and let the owl show her what he saw.

A half-dozen troops in German army uniforms: one sergeant, one corporal, four privates, all armed, pointing their rifles at the deuce and the men in the front seat.

She sighed. Leave it up to the little witch girl. She *called*, and birds answered. More owls, a couple night herons (maybe they were closer to Venice than she thought?), even several nightjars, trilling creakily. She *requested* (never demand, never force) that they swoop down at the Germans. The owls stooped eagerly, fearsome talons forward, and the others followed, if not quite as aggressively.

She heard pistol shots from the front seat, Lieutenant Hirsch and the other two men taking advantage of the bird attack, and *saw* the Germans fall.

"Might as well come out," Lieutenant Hirsch said after a moment, leaning back from the front seat over the bed of the truck.

Frankie shoved the tarp back. "Hi," she said. "You're lucky I'm here."

He smiled briefly. "I suppose we are. Have you been checking for your sister from back there?"

"Tried once or twice. No luck."

He checked his watch. "It's five til nine. We'll wait."

DOTTY FIGURED IT was well past eight, past curfew, given the paucity of civilians along the streets and walkways. She was grateful for the fog that kept her hidden from patrols enforcing the evening curfew, as she slipped along the canals, heading ever outwards towards the lagoon, listening for the church bells. She heard the peals that announced a quarter til, then tucked herself into a recessed doorway of a palazzo that was east of Saint Mark's, just a stone's throw from the lagoon. She let her thoughts wing outward, seeking, pushing herself more than she ever had before. Her head ached, both from being beaten earlier and from her current efforts.

But she had to connect with *something*, something her sister Frankie could reach. Or else none of this meant anything.

There. An owl.

But owls were beyond her. A nightingale, something small, maybe even a fish-eating heron: those were within her capabilities. A bird of prey? Never had she even dreamed she could reach one of those creatures.

She had to try. *Navi,* she projected. *Per favore?* Please? Her temples blossomed with new pain, and she could feel fresh blood trickling from her nose.

Dong. Dong. Dong.

Per favore? Please, please, please....

~

"I GOT SOMETHING!" Frankie said, clutching Hirsch's hand. Brown and cream feathers, piercing yellow eyes, a head that swiveled in her direction.

An owl? An *owl*, from Dotty?

Regardless, Frankie *projected* back, blasting the night sky like a series of flares.

Now they just had to wait.

~

ONE AND A HALF DAYS LATER, March 21st, 1945, Frankie and Dotty sat together in the office at the Cervia Airbase, holding hands tightly, listening to the ongoing reports from the No. 250th RAF Squadron as they approached Venice.

The squadron destroyed not only multiple cargo ships, but an Ariete class torpedo ship and the underwater training facility for German frogmen.

None of the *human* Venetians, watching and cheering from their windows, balconies, and rooftops, were harmed.

The only losses?

A few windows, close to the harbor.

Two pigeons from the flock on the Piazza San Marco. A half dozen rats, residents of the Palazzetto de Verre.

Dotty mourned their sacrifice, the rats and the pigeons.

But she could never tell the survivors, even if she ever wanted to go back to Venice.

Her gift of communication with the little animals, what some called vermin, was also gone.

The stress of contacting the owl was just too much for her over-taxed gift.

To Dotty, it was all worth it.

THE SALT SIDE OF BRASS

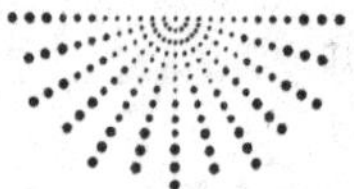

You can't scream underwater, but Jolene was sure trying, clamping her lips around her regulator, biting down on the mouthpiece, and going "Mrrrr! Mrrr!" as loud as she could. Which was about as effective as giving a pig a bath then sending it back to its mudpen.

She'd seen some pretty weird stuff, *really* weird stuff given her gift of the Sense, her ability to go *sideways* or *down* to see the Otherworld.

She wasn't using the Sense now.

And the sight of a severed hand with a cheap Casio digital wristwatch strapped tightly around its hairy wrist was not what she was expecting on her first scuba dive at Casino Point, Catalina Island.

JOLENE DRAGGED the black plastic wheeled case down the boat ramp from the Catalina Express catamaran onto the dock at Avalon, Catalina Island, praying to the sweet lord above that she didn't roll it off the edge. Heavy and unwieldy, the case contained two oxygen tanks, a wetsuit, and various other dive gear. She wasn't a fully certified scuba diver yet, and if the case went over into the drink, she wasn't going to be able to go after it. Not yet, anyways. And definitely not in her cute little sundress over her swim suit. That water was darn cold.

She'd inherited the scuba gear after the death of her most recent client, and close friend, Samantha, a retired high school teacher and diving aficionado. Sam had always wanted to get Jolene scuba diving, and Jolene felt she owed it to the memory of her friend to try.

Despite the fact that really creepy scary things lived in the water.

The wooden mako shark pendant on its black silk cord quivered at the base of her throat in reassurance. He seemed pretty excited about the whole diving thing, her otherworldly protector, her *aumakua*, from Hawai'i. She'd promised him a trip to the Big Island once she was certified.

This trip, getting her final open water dives, was the last step in getting that initial certification. She'd done fine on everything up til now: overcoming mild claustrophobia when encased within the restrictive 7mm neoprene wetsuit, complete with a 5mm hood, to protect against the butt cold California water; all the math and physics and tests; the hours of swimming laps, getting comfortable in the water. She hadn't known how to swim before. Lakes and ponds in East Texas usually featured cottonmouths or gators. Or both.

She'd hired a private instructor, Ken Drews, to teach her how to scuba dive. He had over twenty years of scuba experience, starting with Navy SEAL training, and was patient but matter of fact. He was also big on education. She was getting a deeper introduction to diving than most beginner courses covered. In his late forties, at six foot three, with a lean muscular build, he maintained a laser focus on his health and fitness, which she respected. She herself didn't do anything halfway, so they were a good match as teacher and pupil.

Despite her trepidation and the hard work, she was enjoying diving, more than she'd ever dreamed. *Thank you, Sam.*

She was meeting Ken for her final checkout dives at Casino Point, a protected underwater marine park at the north end of Avalon, right behind the Casino. The Casino wasn't for gambling: rather, the 1920s building included a theater, ballroom, and more. Someday she intended on taking one of the guided tours.

The dock area was packed with tourists getting off the huge catamaran, some divers like her, others ready to just enjoy time on the island.

She could smell popcorn and salt water taffy, making her mouth water, even though she'd had a hearty breakfast burrito before the boat ride, scrambled eggs and cheese and potatoes, dowsed with hot salsa. She worked out all the time and her metabolism was fast. Diving would accentuate that, with the cold water.

Afterwards. She could have a treat afterwards. Maybe a nice big ice cream cone. Mint chocolate chip on a waffle cone.

Ken was already waiting for her at Casino Point, gear arranged on a mat laid out on the asphalt, near the concrete steps, the lower algae-covered, that went down into the water. A few other divers were setting up as well, lucky folks either on vacation or with a flexible schedule like hers, able to dive during the workweek.

Jolene had her own private investigation business, and relished being able to set her own schedule. One of the many benefits. Never mind she was able to use her two special gifts doing her job: the ability to communicate with little animals, rats and pigeons and such, and the Sense, the ability to shift herself, her senses, into the Otherworld, by going *sideways* for a quick look-see, or *down* for detailed examination.

Magic existed, and it wasn't always kind, and sometimes it reached into the real world. That's when she found most of her clients, touched by something just not right.

"Good morning!" Ken said. "Ready to go?"

"Yes, sir," she said, already gyrating into her wetsuit, yanking it up over her bathing suit. They geared up quickly, both doing safety checks on the other.

Ken went into lecture mode.

"Okay, on our first dive, we're going enter at the steps—be careful, they're slippery, and time your entry with the surge so it takes you out —then head north to Octopus Rock, then swing back around, take the time to do some drills. If you're good on air after that, we'll check out the Jacques Cousteau memorial. We'll come back up the steps. We shouldn't be going more than 40 or 50 feet deep. Keep an eye out for Garibaldi, Sheephead, and Kelp bass. Any questions?"

She shook her head.

"Okay, let's go," he said.

Into the drink. She already had two shore dives, near the Redondo Pier last week, but this was special, off a small island in the middle of the ocean. She could feel her heart speed up, a thick pulsing in her chest. Intellectually she acknowledged Catalina was only twenty miles offshore, but it felt in the middle of nowhere right now, as she sank into the clear cold water, bubbles burbling up in front of her mask from her initial rapid breaths. *Slow down, slow down*, she thought. She could feel her mako amulet quiver reassuringly at her throat. If she didn't control her breathing, she was going to use all her air up too fast.

The olive green fronds of kelp surged with the waves. Little fish darted back and forth. She caught a flash of bright orange, an adult Garibaldi, in the kelp forest ahead of her, as she sank deeper. She could taste the brininess on her lips, closed around her regulator. Didn't want to think what else she was tasting. Everything peed and pooped in the ocean.

She pinched her nose and blew out, equalizing the pressure in her ears.

Fifteen feet, twenty, twenty five. The water was still gloriously clear, but the colors were becoming more muted, a blue gray cast over everything.

What would it look like, if she went *sideways* or even *down*? She was sorely tempted.

Safety first, though. Once she gained more experience, maybe, just maybe she'd try that. But she was so vulnerable when she used the Sense. She had to close her eyes and really focus, to remove herself from seeing or feeling or smelling or hearing the real world, for way longer than she wanted, before being able to open her eyes and *see*. Pragmatism and caution and calculation. That was her.

And right now, she had to focus on Ken, swimming gracefully ahead of her.

Another few minutes of adjusting her breathing and bobbing up and down before getting herself to neutral buoyancy, staying at one level in the water, arms tucked against her belly, just using her fins to push herself along. It was just like hiking through the piney forests and limestone stream beds near her granny's house in East Texas. Except she was a little bird, flying through the trees. A veritable forest of kelp. She hadn't understood that until now, when she was actually winding her way between the tall stalks, stretching towards the surface and life-giving sunlight. Fishes flitting around like birds in the canopy.

And so quiet. All she could hear was her own breathing.

Ken stopped at an open sandy spot about thirty feet down. He led her through drills: clearing her mask (flooding it with water than breathing out to get all the water out); taking it off fully and replacing it and clearing again; taking off her tanks and dive vest, and putting them back on. They ended up by practicing buddy breathing, taking turns breathing through just Ken's regulator.

Thumbs up from Ken. Jolene sighed in relief, bubbles tickling her face. The rest of the dive was just for fun. Ken led her through more kelp forest, pointing out tiny Spanish Shawl nudibranchs, purple bodies with frilly orange tentacles, attached to kelp leaves; a huge male Sheephead fish, nearly three feet long, black with a reddish orange band around its belly, gazing at them with solemn red eyes under its bulging brow; and a myriad of smaller kelp bass, pale orangey-gray with white spots and spiny fins.

Finally they reached the underwater memorial, a brass plaque, green with age, embedded in a large rock, surrounded by a jumble of smaller rocks. Ken motioned her to go closer and to read it, while he poked around nearby. She wiped away spots of algae, then hovered above the plaque. *Jacques Cousteau. 1910 to 1997.* A good long life.

An odd glint caught her eye down at the base of rock. Not a fish, not a shell, not natural. Something partially covered by sand, disturbed by her novice finning stirring up the water and sand. She swam down to it. Something was wedged in between the larger, plaque-bearing rock and one of the smaller rocks. She waved at the sand just above the item, causing an eddy that shifted the sand.

And uncovered a cheap Casio digital watch face.

Still running.

Attached to a hairy, severed wrist.

She began gesturing wildly, trying to get Ken's attention. Screaming around her regulator, clenched in her teeth.

He noticed her alarm, swimming directly to her, his eyes following the direction of her finger, pointing at the hand. His eyes widened, and he gestured for her to surface.

They swam back to the steps, steadily and slowly swimming upwards, til they'd taken long enough to surface safely.

"Holy Mary Mother of God," Jolene gasped, blowing her nose, post-dive snot spraying everywhere, slipping her way up the algae-covered steps backwards. She hung onto the railing to steady herself. No way did she want to go back in the water, not with a piece of a person down there.

"Hang on. I'm going to call the police," Ken said. "Phone's in the locker, so just get some water and a snack if you can eat. I have some pretzels and turkey jerky in my backpack." He took off his dive vest and tanks, pulled the heavy wetsuit down around his waist, then jogged off to the line of lockers.

Jolene pulled down her wetsuit top, then crouched on the mat and dug out some turkey jerky and a bottle of water.

And shrieked, an annoying high pitched girly shriek that embarrassed the crap out of her, when someone tapped on her shoulder. A seagull, tentatively walking nearer to beg for a nibble of jerky, flew off in a flurry of wings and fishy smelling seagull poop.

"Good morning," Iggy said. Same ageless, narrow features, long dark hair, bright amber eyes as the last time she saw him a couple months ago. Tall and lean with a new golden tan, he looked like a part-timer of the bustling seaside town, someone who would rent a berth in the harbor for his sailboat. He wore khaki cargo shorts, flip flops, and a faded blue t-shirt advertising glass bottom boat tours, the most casual attire Jolene had ever seen him in. Jolene didn't quite know who or what he was, some sort of sea god, if not a personification of the ocean itself. She'd worked for him in the past, though, and those jobs always involved death and heartbreak.

"You scared me," Jolene said.

Iggy smirked. "Not as much as the first time we met."

He was becoming more human, the more she interacted with him. Then he had to go and remind her of that night in her garage, when she thought she was going to be drowned by the vengeful sea. Or torn apart by a shark-toothed humanoid sea monster, i.e. Iggy himself.

Though she hadn't called him Iggy then.

"There were more pieces than just the hand," he said. "My people ate most of them. The bones are scattered. But that piece was warded, so they let it be. Did you *look* at it?"

"Are you crazy? Of course I didn't," she said.

"You need to." A touch of the old Iggy, stern and implacable. The Sea God.

"I just came up from my dive. I need to wait at least an hour, to outgas nitrogen—"

He grasped her by the shoulders and yanked her against him, placing his mouth on hers and inhaling.

"No, you don't," he said, releasing her. "You're back to normal. Human and frail and with an air breather's normal chemistry."

She shuddered, wiping her mouth. "Hon, in this day and age, you don't just accost a woman like that." Creepy, totally creepy, and back totally in the inhuman camp. She could feel her mako quivering in outrage at her throat.

He touched the pendant. "Interesting," he said. "Now, go *look*."

~

SHE GEARED UP, swapping out her old tank for a fully filled tank, running through the checklists, and headed back down the slippery steps. Ken was still on the phone, gesturing wildly, as she entered the water. She really hoped she wasn't screwing her chances of getting certified. A solo dive? Let alone one without adequate time between dives? He'd be right to fail her.

But she couldn't say no to Iggy. Her granny had taught her to be careful of Otherworldly beings, and as much as diving back down to the hand and using the Sense underwater scared her, standing up to Iggy seemed like a far scarier option.

She descended rapidly. She didn't want to be down here any longer than she had to.

Something tugged gently on her fin. She yanked her foot away, then turned, hovering in the water. Iggy. Somehow outfitted with complete dive gear. He gave her an okay sign, then swam in front of her, leading her to the memorial.

Swimming in his wake was effortless. She was gently tugged along, slipping swiftly between stalks of kelp, not even coming close to becoming entangled in the fronds.

They reached the memorial. The hand was fully exposed, still pristine, the watch face reflecting pale sunlight.

Iggy placed his hand on her shoulder and squeezed, nodding.

She nodded back, then closed her eyes.

Down.

The water felt, if not warmer, more comforting, more a part of her. She could feel her mako shake loose of the silk cord around her neck.

Down.

She could hear faint singing, deep bass tones that rolled through her belly, higher pitched squeaks and clacks.

Down.

She opened her eyes and gasped, her regulator floating out of her mouth. She grabbed it and bit down hard on the mouthpiece.

Glorious colors. The blue cast was gone. The olive green of the kelp was as rich as velvet, the Garibaldi so bright an orange they looked like miniature suns. Jolene could see nudibranchs like pieces of mobile jewelry climbing on the kelp, amethyst and citrine. A leopard shark swam lazily by, her brown spots vibrant against her cream colored body. A sea lion nipped at her fins, laughing at her with its rich brown eyes, mouth open in a surprisingly canine grin, before swimming away.

Starfish, bright orange, inched along the sand. Purple sea urchins, their spines tipped with little glowing lights, nestled together on the rocks.

The rocks. The memorial itself glowed faintly, all the patina of age and algae wiped away. "The sea loved him," whispered Iggy.

Her mako swam between her and the rocks, bigger than she'd ever seen him, at least five feet long. Almost as big as her five foot six. He seemed happy, his sharky toothy grin wide.

Until he saw the hand. He positioned himself between it and Jolene, and wouldn't let her past. She had to hold his dorsal fin, snug herself up against his body, to get a better look at the hand.

The fingers were twitching, just a little, so little that at first Jolene thought it was just a trick of the current. Then the hand clenched into a fist.

She didn't scream. But she did squeak. She could see the tendons twitching in the stump as the hand straightened out. Oh, that just ain't right. Zombie hand. She glanced at Iggy.

He was all Sea-Lord fancy, gills fluttering at his neck, lambent orange eyes brighter than the Garibaldi, scaled body lean and elegant, thin phosphorescent stripes streaking across like the glow of a ctenophore's cilia. Sort of *Shape of Water* mesmerizing. He nodded at her, gave a diver's okay sign, a human touch for an inhuman presence.

The hand began inching towards her like a starfish. Her mako was trembling like a pissed off pit bull. If he could growl, she'd been hearing an earful. She patted his side, trying to calm him down, past herself freaking out.

The hand took advantage of her distraction. It had snuck a few feet closer, fingertips wiggling. She couldn't help herself. She backed away, sculling with her hands to shift back a foot or two without taking her eyes off the hand.

It held up its index finger. *Wait.*

To her right, Iggy was waving his narrow hands around, hissing words into the water. A glimmer started at the severed wrist, the ghostly outline of a forearm, then the upper arm, then the rest of the body.

Clothed, thank the sweet lord for the tiniest of blessings. A young man in faded ripped up blue jeans, a black heavy metal band t-shirt, and worn combat boots sat up in the sand, looking at his solid hand, then at the shimmery outline that was the rest of him. He had straight black hair, razored short on the sides and back, but long on top so that in air it would flop over. In the water it just waved back and forth with the current. His skin had the pallor of death, a sallow tan, and his eyes glowed an otherworldly silver. His cheeks were pocked with faint acne scars, but otherwise he was sweet-featured and boyish, with full lips. Boy-band handsome.

Too young to end up scattered in pieces over the ocean floor.

Hey, querida, he said, smiling at her, those silvery eyes taking in her trim form even in the thick wetsuit. Flirting!

Exasperation overruled her fear.

Who did this to you? she projected. She'd never communicated with a human this way before. Only with the little animals, rats and pigeons and such. But she couldn't outright talk underwater, and she was pretty sure she'd just heard him in her head, so it was worth a try. And he wasn't really human anymore if he was dead, right?

He cocked his head. *Did what?*

Killed you and cut you into pieces, she said. Oh, her granny must be rolling in her grave at Jolene's bluntness. But Jolene didn't have a lot of time before she'd have to surface. Her gauge was showing just a few more minutes before she'd have to start swimming back up. She was going through air like crazy.

The boy's silver eyes widened, widened until they were like twin moons, anime huge, and he screamed.

And disappeared. All of him, even the hand.

Except the watch. It sank down the sand, rocking back and forth in the current.

Jolene shoved past her mako, swam forward, and grabbed the watch. Her mako shrank until she could tuck the little wooden form into a pocket on her dive vest. She held her other hand out to Iggy, trusting him to keep her safe, and closed her eyes.

Up. Up. Up.

"WHAT WERE YOU THINKING?" Iggy said, back in full wetsuit, helping her get her tank and dive vest off, letting her assist him in turn. "Telling that poor child—"

"What were you thinking?" bellowed Ken, running up to her. "Are you crazy? Did you just go dive into what's going to be a crime scene? By yourself?"

"Iggy was with me. Iggy, meet Ken, etc."

Iggy held his hand to Ken. "Delighted," he said.

"Do I know you?" Ken said.

"I'm a friend of Jolene's," Iggy said. "But maybe we've met in the past. In fact, I'm sure we have. Navy SEAL?"

A friend? That was a better gift than a basketful of fluffy orange kittens. Jolene wasn't ever going to let Iggy forget he said that.

"Twenty years ago," Ken said.

"Ken, I'm really sorry, but I had to go look at it again," Jolene interrupted. "Something seemed off. Iggy volunteered to dive with me. Turned out it was just a mannequin hand, just left down there to freak out people. Can you call the police, let them know it was just a bad joke?"

"Here's the hand," Iggy offered, holding out a lifelike, but definitely plastic, hand.

"There was a watch," Ken said.

"Fell off. Sorry," Jolene said. She felt her face burning. Oh, she hated to lie. Liars were lowest of the low. Down there with folks who abused animals and kids.

Ken glared at her suspiciously.

"I saw it fall, I just wasn't quick enough to grab it," said Iggy.

"Hm. Alright, let me call. Shower up, we'll grab lunch, then we can do one last dive. Iggy, would you like to join us?"

"I'd be pleased," said Iggy.

~

KEN HAD GONE to the bathroom, leaving Iggy and Jolene alone in the boat, the booth that was set up in an actual boat in the corner of the Lobster Trap. Jolene finished up the last of her mahi tacos and onion rings, wondering if she could get away with ordering a side of garlic bread. Someone within smelling distance had some, and she was still hungry.

Iggy was staring at the decorations. Swordfish on the wall, a giant fish hanging from the ceiling under the skylight, the antlers on a post near the bar. "I get the fish," he said over the noisy chitchat of the other diners, "but why the antlers?"

"Dunno," Jolene said. "First time here. Before I head off to the little mermaid's room, spill. What was that and what can we do?"

"No Pissy Attitudes," Iggy read the sign over the bar. "That means you, too, Jolene."

"Regardless." She stared at him.

He waved his hand. "Obviously murdered, obviously not at rest. You can't fix everything, Jolene."

"You had me try to fix what happened with Patrick." Patrick was a murdered selkie; Iggy had sent her north to solve his murder.

"Patrick was one of mine."

"And this boy—"

"Seriously, Jolene, you would like to tell me that poor Latino boy is yours? You're a white, upper middle class woman from Texas. I've travelled everywhere the ocean touches, Jolene, and I know how boys like that are treated. Especially where you're from, by people who look like you."

"Not by me," Jolene said.

"Pshaw. If you saw him on the street, alive...well, you wouldn't even notice him."

"I'm not going to argue about this," Jolene said. "I want to at least find out who he is. If he has family, they deserve to know. You said his hand was warded. That brings the Otherworld into it, and since it happened in your domain, you're involved."

Ken came back to the booth. "Ready to get your last dive done?" he asked.

"Yes, sir," Jolene said, pushing her chair back.

"So nice to run into you," Iggy said, standing and shaking Ken's hand.

"Same here, man. Jolene?"

"Let's go. Iggy, I'll call you later."

THE LAST DIVE was just for fun. They dove down to the Kismet, a small sailboat, and the adjacent upside-down glass bottom boat, at around sixty five feet deep. "We'll do the SueJac next time," Ken told her after they were done. "It goes down to around ninety feet. Really neat wreck. She got blown out and dashed against the rocks and sank during the Santa Ana winds. They actually extended the park boundaries to included her."

Jolene paused in packing up her case. "So I'm certified?"

"Yep. I'll get the process started with your cards ASAP. Your two dives today went great."

"What about the end of the first dive?" she asked.

"What about it? No problems I could tell."

Iggy. Iggy must've done something to him.

She trundled her case back towards the dock, taking a break halfway there at the public showers, washing the salt out of her hair and the sand out of, well, everywhere. She pulled on a pair of blue jeans and a navy cotton gansey-style sweater her granny had knit for her. The sun was getting lower in the sky, and the temperature dropping, even though it was nearly June. She tucked her mako amulet, back on its silk cord, under the sweater. She strapped the boy's watch onto her wrist.

The Catalina Express trip back to the port at San Pedro took at least an hour.

More than enough time to go *down* and see what she could from the watch.

~

SHE FOUND a quiet corner on the inside of the catamaran on the lowest deck. It wasn't as busy as earlier, and no one ended up sitting near her.

She didn't waste time, taking the watch off and holding in both hands.

Down, down, down.

She opened her eyes. The interior of the ship was dark. The watch glowed, just a little. She frowned. She needed something, darn it. She poked it, tapped on the scratched face, wiggled it. Nothing.

She licked her finger then swiped across the top of the face. It brightened briefly.

Crapola. She tore at a hangnail til blood welled up, and wiped a few garnet drops across the face.

The watch face shone like a beacon.

"Show me," she breathed.

Everything went black. But she could hear. Voices, men arguing, harsh breathing. Her breathing...or rather, Angel's breathing. He had a pillowcase over his head, and his hands were cuffed behind him. His legs were tied to the chair legs. He was terrified, his heart rate so fast she didn't know how it just didn't burst.

Angel. She had a first name. Check missing persons' reports, and that might be enough. She struggled, trying to go *up*, not wanting to be around for what was going to happen next.

"What happens next?" he whispered, struggling against the cuffs.

Up.

But he kept her there, with him.

"Let me go," Jolene said.

"*Querida*? What happens next?" His voice was soft but rich, the panic controlled. She thought of his boy band handsome face. The voice suited.

"Boy band? Really? Pretty lady, that is an insult. Sepultura is more my style."

"I can't help you," Jolene said. "I can't stop what happened."

"I guess I don't walk away."

"I can tell your family. So you're not just missing. They'll never know otherwise." Not when there was nothing left anywhere to find, let alone identify.

"Angel Ortega," he said after a moment. "Angel Jose Ortega." She could hear the voices in the background yelling louder. Closer. She didn't have much time. Angel didn't have much time.

"Why are you here? Why do they want to kill you?"

"Wrong place, wrong time," he said.

"Angel, they will kill you."

"I was helping my uncle with a cleaning job, an office building. One of his crew was sick. I saw some paperwork, permits, some notes about it. It was wrong, so I took pictures—"

The men were there. She could feel the heat of their nearness on Angel's bare forearms. It was too late.

Up.

"If I tell them, will they let me go?" he asked desperately. To the men: "I didn't see anything, I'm sorry, just let me go—"

She felt it, felt the cut that slashed through the front of his shirt, slicing into the skin of his chest.

They would never let him go. They would chop him into pieces and scatter them, all except for his hand. Why would they ward it?

Right now that didn't matter.

Another slice, parallel to the first. She heard Angel cry out. She could feel blood soaking her navy sweater.

She couldn't bear to let them torture this boy. Her granny had told her stories of her Great Aunt Dotty, in World War 2, how she'd been a spy. How she'd used her gifts to get intel, reports, to the Allies.

How she'd accidentally killed a pigeon, being too forceful. Be gentle, her granny had admonished. Don't ever do what Aunt Dotty did.

Sorry. She was so sorry.

ANGEL! she blasted. Never, never had she ever projected so loudly. If she normally was a one on the Richter Scale, this was a ten. Exponential. Blood dripped out of her nose and she felt dizzy. She could feel him convulse. Hear the furious howls of the men, as they lost their victim.

Up. Up up up—

Jolene *felt* Angel die as she broke free. *Up.*

She opened her eyes.

A little girl, blond hair in neat pigtails, wearing a flowered sundress, stood in front of her. "You're crying," she said to Jolene.

"Something really sad happened," Jolene said. She felt her sweater. Damp. She looked at her fingers. No blood. Her chest ached, though. She wanted to throw up.

But she had a name.

~

SHE DOUBLE CHECKED THE ADDRESS. This was it. A neatly kept stucco 1950s home, freshly painted a medium blue, with a white-painted wrought iron fence. A jacaranda tree had dropped purple flowers all over the concrete walk to the front porch. Beyond the musky odor of the flowers she could smell meat cooking, fragrant with citrus and chile.

She knocked on the heavy duty screen door. The front door opened, revealing a woman in her forties with Angel's full lips and high cheekbones.

"I need to tell you what happened to Angel," Jolene said, holding out the watch.

It was all she could do.

For now.

THE SACRIFICE OF THE MODERN WORLD

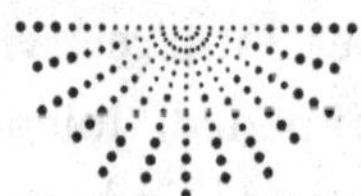

Rotten fish and cotton candy and seagull poop: the smell of the boardwalk by Redondo Pier. Especially on warm summer weekend days, when tourists swarmed the pier area and dropped their snacks and sodas on the concrete, attracting even more seagulls and subsequently more seagull poop.

But Jolene preferred the boardwalk as is, in all its tawdry glory, to it becoming gentrified and downright boring, filled with the upscale clothing shops and restaurant chains that you could find in any Southern California beach town overcome by developer greed.

Her favorite taproom, boasting over a hundred beers on draft (and she wasn't talking Bud Light), with its sticky concrete floor and rickety stools and tables, wouldn't stick around longer than a greased pig if the Pier got developed. The fried fish and fresh crab shops would be bought out and replaced by farm-to-table bistros, the arcade torn down and who knows put what put in its place.

She'd heard that someone was approaching the city to redevelop the area by the old power plant; every once in awhile that came up during city elections. But the Pier seemed safe.

On the topic of pier eateries ... she had a hankering for some sweet fresh crab right now. Didn't matter that it was barely past breakfast time. She'd had a hard workout this morning, lifting weights then running three miles down along the beach on the hard packed sand. She didn't work out to have a bikini body even though she was a tanned, slim, blue-eyed blonde. She worked out because being strong and fast might make the difference between alive or dead.

But working out that hard sure did raise a hunger.

She checked her watch, with its vintage Cinderella face and a stretch metal band. It had been her momma's when her momma was a little girl. Her momma had never given up on the idea of princesses being saved by handsome princes, which accounted for the parade of low-life boyfriends during Jolene's early childhood.

Thank the good lord for her granny, who took charge and raised her, teaching her right from wrong, how to keep her head on straight, and most importantly, how to deal with her two strange gifts. The first was the ability to communicate with the little animals, rats and pigeons and seagulls and the like. The second, the Sense, let her mentally step *down* or *sideways* to see, smell, and hear the traces of magic and the Otherworld that was just there at the edges. It wasn't without risk: every time she let it take control she made herself more and more vulnerable, and more apt to lose herself.

Anyhow, fifteen minutes til she was supposed to meet her client, an old friend, with a brand new case just for Jolene. She had time to grab a little somethin' if she hurried.

JOLENE WIPED the last bit of clarified butter and crab bits from her chin, hoping Sam wouldn't notice the grease spot on her snug-fitting black tank top once Jolene gave Sam the sandwich she'd picked up for her. She tossed the last crust of bread from her sandwich to a hopeful seagull, smiling at its excited squawks.

She hustled towards Jeannie's Shell Shoppe on the Pier proper. Didn't want to be late. She prided herself on her professionalism. Even if the client was a friend, and despite the food on her shirt.

The Redondo Beach Pier had several sections. One was the

International Boardwalk area, with a small rectangular marina, a crane for hoisting boats into dry dock, her beloved taproom, the arcade, and various fish and crab shops, all boxed in by the multilevel parking structure on two sides.

A more modern, recently updated concrete pier arced out at the mouth of the marina opening out over the water and headed south, thus enclosing a bit of beach, off limits to swimmers. No shops on it, just benches and a few tables for people to relax at. And a great view out past the breakwater. You could watch for dolphins and sea lions or be entertained by the pelicans and cormorants for hours.

The far end of that section connected to the old wooden pier: more restaurants and some super kitschy souvenir shops, including Jeannie's Shell Shoppe.

As far as kitsch went, Jeannie's was one of the better shops. Yes, it had its selection of glue-gun shelled mermaids, sea lions, and other critters (some even with googly eyes), but it also boasted bins upon bins of shells from all around the world. Tables and shelves filled with shells. You could take a little basket and go from bin to bin, picking out your favorites, squeezing between the closely packed in tables, breathing in the salt from exotic locales far, far away. Whelk, cowrie, turban, cone shells. Jolene had to admit she was a bit of a magpie, and usually bought something to add to the bowl of shells she kept in her bathroom. She would dream about white sand beaches in Fiji or Bora Bora or all the other places she'd never been, just from touching those shells.

Anyhow, the original Jeannie was long since buried, and her daughter Sam, Samantha Crispen, a retired high school Earth sciences teacher, now ran the shop. Jolene had met her once at a Chamber of Commerce mixer a couple years ago. They hit it off, Jolene respecting Sam's scrappiness and intellect, and Sam the same for Jolene, and they both took the time to have coffee together at least three weeks out of every four. Sam had lived a fascinating life: degrees in Geology and Vulcanology, research all along the coast, Hawai'i, and up to the northern edge of the Ring of Fire, until she decided to get married, have a kid, and tackle teaching ninth graders. Which Sam always told Jolene was the most difficult thing she'd ever done, hands down.

Jolene didn't get called in on run-of-the-mill private investigation cases. Word got around she was the gal to contact if things went weird. So she was more than a bit curious when Sam called her the day before, an undercurrent of panic in her soft voice, to hire her.

"You know I'm hoping to pass the store on to my son this year," Sam said after Jolene arrived promptly at ten a.m. "But not if things like this are happening." She'd locked the front door, turned the sign to CLOSED, before escorting Jolene to the tiny office in back, her slim back ramrod straight with tension, stress visible even under a loose-fitting sundress that highlighted her tanned skin and whipcord muscles.

There was barely room for the small pine tabletop with its laptop computer and coffee pot, resting on a dorm-sized fridge and a filing cabinet, let alone the two of them, but Jolene squeezed into the turquoise folding chair that Sam offered. A couple of scuba tanks sat in one corner, with diving gear neatly stacked next to them. A wetsuit was draped over the back of Sam's vintage wooden desk chair. Mounds of reference books and field guides, for tidal invertebrates and fish as well as shells, teetered on the corner of the desk. Sam stacked the books on the floor under the desk between the fridge and file cabinet, then snagged two chipped coffee cups from the window ledge behind her and filled them.

"Sorry, no sugar or cream. I had some half and half but it went bad, haven't replaced it yet." Sam said, sitting down behind the desk, offering a cup to Jolene. "Anyways, I had Mike do his first buying run a month ago. Hawai'i, Fiji, French Polynesia. Most of the time we just order from suppliers online, but sometimes, we do go after something unique. Sculptures, real works of art from local artists. We received the shipment from his trip last week, and since then, things have been, well, weird."

"Weird?"

Sam nodded, hazel eyes darkening in worry. "At first it was just little things out of place. I just thought it was me, a case of CRS syndrome—"

"CRS?" Jolene took a sip of coffee. She preferred cream and sugar, but boy, this was tasty.

"Can't remember shit. Just wait til you get older, Jolene." Sam's smirk didn't quite reach her eyes." Anyways, at first it was just a shell sculpture in a slightly different spot, or bin tags swapped. Little things. Then I would come in to find shells arranged on the checkout counter in different geometric patterns."

Self-deprecation aside, Jolene didn't consider Sam old. Sam was as sharp as they come, and Jolene had read about her in the online archives of the Daily Breeze, the local newspaper, after they first met, read about how sad the high school community was sad that she was retiring, an award-winning teacher of more than thirty years. And Sam kept herself fit, fit enough to shore dive in Redondo's cold water, making it past the waves to dive down into Redondo Canyon. Fitter than most twenty year olds. Jolene didn't think Sam's mind was slipping any more than her body.

"Yesterday morning, when I came in, the tables in the middle of the store were all shoved to the sides. And this was on the floor." She held out her cell phone to Jolene. "I took a picture. I did call the police, because of the marine mammal protection act. And it was so disturbing." *And I was scared*, her face said.

The photo showed a spiral of sea shells radiating outward, sea shells of all sizes and colors, from iridescent abalone near the center to tiny, multi-colored Gould's Wedge clam shells you could find on any Southern California beach, at the edge. The pattern filled the bulk of the store's floor, with all the display tables pushed aside.

And in the center sat the severed head of a sea lion, its eyes milky, in a pool of tacky drying blood.

Well, that was uglier than a toy poodle picking a fight with a gator.

The sea lion head had been taken to the Marine Mammal Care Center in San Pedro for a necropsy. Jolene figured she'd go there after finishing up at the Shell Shoppe.

Sam had a small security camera system, but though it worked perfectly during the daytime with no changes to the settings or a even reboot, the nighttime recordings from around 9 p.m. to 4 a.m. just showed a blank screen for each night. No help there, other than the acknowledgement that whatever was doing thing had both the capacity to recognize that there was a security system, and the ability to affect it. Something that knew the modern world.

The police had checked for physical evidence, for fingerprints at least on the window frames and doors, and so on, but in a commercial space, that didn't mean much. The Shell Shoppe wasn't ever swamped with customers, but a steady stream kept the place in business. There was no evidence of any tampering with the locks, nothing to suggest a forced entry.

"And nothing is missing?" Jolene asked.

"Not that I can tell," said Sam.

"And what was in this shipment?"

Sam stood up. "Some of it's in the storage room here, some of it in our storage unit in Torrance. I haven't had a chance to unpack it all yet."

The storage room was the mirror of the office in size, at the opposite corner of the back of the shop (a tiny bathroom with just a toilet and a stainless steel sink Jolene suspected was for a boat's bathroom took up the space in between the office and storage room). Wire racks were filled with boxes and bins. A plastic-topped table sat under the back window, several boxes stacked up on it, the top one opened.

"That one has some particularly lovely pieces from Hawai'i. Some old pieces from different archaeological sites, some new. It's all legal," Sam added defensively.

"Show me the older items," Jolene said. How many times did some good-intentioned person end up with a cursed item? Happened all the time with her cases, she had to admit. All the time.

She supposed she couldn't blame folks. After all, the vast majority didn't believe in curses til one bit them right in the behind. She'd never shared her gifts with Sam. How was Same supposed to know curses and fairies and goddesses were real?

Sam took out four different pieces: a stone poi pounder, elegantly curved for such a simple tool; a feathered anklet, strung with shark teeth; a voluptuous wooden idol, depicting what Jolene assumed was a goddess; and a knife-shape wooden piece, studded with shark teeth along the edges.

Jolene closed her eyes. *Sideways*, just a small stutter step, a bob and a dip; she didn't want to go too deep, not yet, not until she determined which of the pieces was the culprit.

She opened her eyes.

The storage room was dim, dimmer than without the Sense, like sunlight filtered down into deep water. She could hear the soft scrub of waves on soft white sand, could feel the vibrations of monsoon raindrops plonking on thick broad leaves, could smell the sweet heady scents of tropical flowers.

But the items, other than glowing with the soft patina of the passage of time, sat on the table with all the magical essence of a road-kill armadillo.

That couldn't be right. *Down*. Deeper.

Off to the corner she thought she saw a skitter of something ducking out of sight behind a box. But the artifacts just sat there. No ghosts or spirits hovering, no ill will or spells oozing out. Not even a touch of divinity from the idol. Nothing.

She closed her eyes. *Up*. Opened her eyes and re-orientated herself to the real world.

"There's nothing strange about these things," Jolene told Sam. "Are there any other artifacts?"

"Nothing old," Sam said. She looked skeptical.

Jolene sighed. "Okay, I'm off to look at that sea lion head."

Sam nodded. "I'll let them know you're on your way. I know the vet there."

THE MARINE MAMMAL CARE CENTER, located in at Fort MacArthur in San Pedro, took care stranded or injured seals and sea lions. Jolene had visited it last spring, just to see the orphaned or abandoned sea lion pups. Visitors were allowed to stand at the chainlink fence and watch volunteers care for the babies in the concrete pools, smaller plastic pools, or concrete pens. The pups were sure cute with their big brown eyes and playful antics, and Jolene, checking a couple months later, was relieved to hear most had been successfully released.

She parked her car, a late eighties baby blue and rust Chevy Nova that she just knew was going to die on her some day (and others would argue it should've been put out to pasture decades ago), in the visitor parking lot.

She breathed in the fresh ocean air, just barely infused by fish, as she got out of her car and headed up the steps to the main building of the Care Center. She could hear barking. It sounded like the place was full. The fishy scent intensified the closer she got. Well, it was what they ate.

A young woman dressed in khaki shorts and a MMMC t-shirt, auburn hair caught up in a pony tail, greeted her as she entered. "Can I help you? If you'd like to see the sea lions, you need to go around the outside—"

"Thanks, but my name is Jolene Tomberlin. I'm a private investigator working for Sam Crispen, the owner of Jeannie's Shell Shoppe."

The woman paled, her freckles standing out against her fair skin. "Oh. The head."

"Yep. The head."

"I'll take you to Dr Jakes."

"Thanks." Jolene followed the woman through the building, out to the back pens, where a group of people decked out in bright yellow plastic aprons stood in a half circle around an older heavyset woman in navy scrubs and knee-high rubber boots, her grey and brown hair tied up in a messy bun.

"Dr Jakes? This is—" she looked at Jolene. The older woman looked over at Jolene.

"Jolene Tomberlin, PI. Working with the Shell Shoppe. Nice to meet you, Dr Jakes," Jolene said.

"Alright, kids, you know your jobs. Get to it," Dr Jakes said to the group. To Jolene: "Follow me."

"I met Sam when she was still teaching," Dr Jakes continued as she led Jolene into the hospital section of the facility, her gait graceful and swift as she navigated plastic pools, ice chests with fish, and buckets of cleaning supplies. "She brought the marine sciences club kids over on a field trips. Haven't seen her in person since she retired, but the Shell Shoppe always donates something for our fundraisers and silent auctions. Sam called when she found the head, and mentioned she was hiring someone, that she wasn't sure the police would be able to explore every angle."

"I tend to look at things a different way," Jolene said.

Dr Jakes opened the door of a large refrigerator, a sticker stating NO ITEMS FOR HUMAN CONSUMPTION emblazoned across it. Jolene peeked in over Dr Jake's shoulder. Vials of medication, trays of vaccines, some tubes filled with what she figured was blood. Ziplocked bags of small whole fish, mackerel or something like it.

Dr Jakes shoved a can of soda and a Chinese food takeout container to the side before grabbing a head-sized garbage bagged item lodged in the back of the bottom shelf.

"Here it is," Dr Jakes said, placing it on the rack covering a metal table and sink combo in the center of the room. "I'm pretty much done with it, studied it all day yesterday after I got it, so once you've done whatever you need to do, it's going in the freezer and will be picked up for cremation later this week."

"What did you find?" asked Jolene. The sea lion's milky eyes seemed to be staring at her. She shivered.

Dr Jakes shrugged. "It looks like something, a shark, chewed off all the body and left the head. Bizarre. I told the police it doesn't look like someone chopped it off. See how it's all jagged and torn?" She pointed to different areas on the severed neck.

"In fact...." Dr Jakes pulled on some latex gloves and picked up a pair of tweezers and began poking around in the muscle, digging a bit deeper, then wiggling something out. "Look here. A tooth." She fished it out proudly, flourishing a very large shark's tooth, about two inches long, bits of sea lion flesh hanging off the serrated edges of the tooth.

Jolene gulped. She usually had a stronger stomach, but this was a bit much.

"And then the fact that it's so well preserved. No insects, no sea parasites, nothing else eating the dead head. Just fascinating." Dr Jakes poked the flesh again.

Thank the sweet lord there weren't any bugs. Or maggots. "I have to do something that may look strange," Jolene said, just wanting to get away from the head as quickly as possible. "I mean, I'm just going to stand here, I don't need or want to touch it. But I just need a few moments."

Dr Jakes looked a bit crestfallen at Jolene's lack of enthusiasm. "Okay," she said.

Jolene braced herself, hands on the edge of the table, and closed her eyes. *Sideways* wasn't going to cut it. She would have to go deep for this. *Down.* Oh, Jolene hated this, because until she got where she was going, she was vulnerable, and she was already spooked by the sea lion's eyes. *Down. Down.*

Then opened her eyes. A star swept night sky twinkled above, the white sand under her feet glimmering in reflection. Phosphorescent tipped waves lapped at her toes. A sharp, vibrating drum beat echoed through her chest. The rustle of skirts hissed around her. And the sea lion head stared at her and barked, barked in time with the drum beat, until the shadow of a shark reared up behind it, like it was riding a huge wave, cutting off the barking. Manō hae, manō hae, fierce shark, fierce shark.

Hungry shark.

The shadow gulped up the sea lion head. Gone, just like that. The drum beat intensified, quickened, as the shadow moved towards her.

Holy Mary Mother of God.

Up, up, up.

Jolene opened her eyes to Dr Jakes, face ashen, saying, "What the fuck, what the fuck."

The sea lion head was gone.

~

A STOP at the Redondo Beach library to do some quick internet research on Oceania legends, religion, and mythology. Mostly the same barebones stuff, repeated word for word on various sites, but she got some insight. She glanced at the community announcements board on the way out, then stopped cold. That developer, James Rhydon, looking at the old power plant? Apparently he wanted to do a bid for work on the Pier. There was a meeting next week at the library for any concerned residents.

She couldn't worry about that now.

Back to the Shell Shoppe. Cotton candy and fish and chips. Jolene's stomach churned. She didn't want to think of food, let alone smell it. She didn't think the shark would stop at sea lions. What would *it* eat next?

Jolene pushed past a couple customers dawdling, poking through various bins, indecisive. Her granny would be disappointed in her rudeness, but Jolene didn't care. Sam was working the register, ringing up the purchases of a mom with two young boys, a bright smile on her face that came nowhere near her hazel eyes.

"Sam, we need to talk. Now," Jolene said as soon at the mother and kids left.

"But—"

"Now. Kick them out," Jolene said, waving a hand at the remaining browsers. "Give them one of those pretty ivory turban shells each as an apology, or whatever, but change that sign to closed."

Sam frowned but complied. Not as quick as Jolene wanted, but she knew Sam was a stubborn woman, to have taught high schoolers for thirty odd years. Sam was just out of her element.

Sideways.

Jolene could hear the scritching of something moving along the floors, could just catch the glimpse of something — *multiple* some-things — scootching under the tables. The Otherworld was closer than it had been even midmorning, and that just wasn't a good thing. Soon those critters would be moving around in the real world. *Ka-poe-kino-pupu* most like, little shell spirits. Sometimes good, sometimes bad. They weren't the issue. Maybe they did some of the redecorating, but they hadn't done anything beyond little tricks.

Ka-poe-kina-manō hae, the spirit of a shark, a hungry, angry shark, far from home, who ate sea lions and wanted more, much more... he was the problem.

And Jolene wasn't sure if she could solve that problem.

"Let me see the new artwork," she said to Sam. They went to the storage room.

Sam carefully unpacked a box. A set of three photographs of crimson lava flowing into the sea, shot from what seemed to be perilous angles for the photographer; an abstract painting in grays and dark blues and reds and fish belly white that she couldn't wrap her head around; and a small carved wooden longfin mako shark about a foot long, stylized but so graceful it looked like it was swimming in the air. Scared as she was of sharks right now, it charmed Jolene with its energy.

"These are all the other pieces," Sam said. "The photographs are by Kai Māhoe, a very talented young photographer on the Big Island. Mike said he found the shark at an outdoor market. One of a kind, sold by a young Hawaiian woman. The painting is by an up and coming artist, Jon Rhydon, from Kona."

Sideways wasn't enough. *Down* just a smidgen.

The photographs glowed red and orange and yellow, filled with the photographer's adoration and worship of Pele, but were otherwise unremarkable in the Otherworld.

The shark smiled at her toothily, but without malice. She'd read about protector sharks, 'aumakua, sharks that would protect a person or a family. She reached out to the sculpture, touching the tip of her finger to its carved teeth. It cut her, no worse than a paper cut, and she let a few drops of blood drip into its mouth. It swallowed the blood, eyeing her contemplatively, then grew in size to about three feet long, the size of a small reef shark. It swam through the air to her, putting itself between her and the last item.

The painting. It wasn't abstract any longer. The painting too had grown, much larger than her shark, larger than the what the storage room should allow, at least ten feet wide by ten feet tall. She could hear, could feel, the sharp deep sound of the pahu drums, the rhythm quickening.

The subject was clearly the open maw of a great white shark, filling the foreground of the painting, serrated teeth trailing bits of bloody flesh. Its dead dark eyes stared at her, and it opened its jaws wider.

And lunged.

Past Jolene, to Sam.

It grabbed Sam, clamping down on her shoulder, her arm in its mouth, pulling her away.

Her shark swam in frenzied circles around Jolene. It could protect her. It just wasn't strong enough to protect Sam too.

Jolene needed more help. A kicked colony of fire ants level of help, boiling over and unstoppable.

A goddess.

Her eyes flickered to the photographs. Could they be a link, a link to Pele? They brightened, the lava glowing more intensely. Jolene could feel the heat, reddening her skin even from several feet away.

"Pele, Pele, Pele," Jolene whispered as Sam screamed, the white shark savagely shaking his head, blood spraying everywhere. Holy Mary Mother of God, she prayed she wasn't bringing in something worse than the white shark and she wasn't about to burn down the Pier. This shark was a devourer, insatiable, but Pele? She was a goddess of destruction.

"Pele, Pele, Pele."

Third time's a charm, especially the third set of three.

"Pele, Pele, Pele."

A tall sturdy young woman appeared between Jolene and the white shark, dressed in a red cotton shift, edged with black at the hem that ebbed and flowed. She smelled of sulfur and ash. A fuzzy white dog with orange eyes pranced at her feet. Her long black hair gleamed with lambent red highlights. Flames, cupped in her left hand, danced eagerly, ready for destruction. Her eyes glowed orange in her dark face, her expression distant.

The white shark paused, Sam hanging limply from its mouth, unconscious, no longer screaming.

"Tutu Pele," Jolene said. "Please, intercede. This greedy shark seeks to devour more than his share." *Rhydon*. The son of the developer James, perhaps? "The white shark is not one of yours."

Tiger sharks, white tips, scalloped hammerheads: those were the common species, living in the waters of Hawai'i. Even her long finned Mako was a pelagic species found near Hawai'i.

Great whites were rare, very rare, in Hawai'i. Interlopers.

Pele glanced over her shoulder at the white shark, then flung her flames at the painting.

The flames fireballed across the painting and the white shark, causing paint, and shark flesh, to blister. The shark let go of Sam but continued thrashing, this time in agony itself.

Jolene didn't know if sharks made any noises in the real world other than splashing, but this one sure as heck did, a shrill shriek that caused her to cover her ears, wishing that horrible screech would just stop.

And it did, eventually. There was nothing left of the shark, or the painting.

But nothing else burned.

Sam's crumpled body, her arm and shoulder mangled, lay on the floor of the storage room.

Pele nodded somberly to Jolene and scooped up Sam's body like she weighed nothing, driftwood on the beach, cradling the old woman to her chest. Pele then disappeared, along with her little white dog.

Up. Tears squeezed past her tightly closed lids. *Up.*

SAM'S BODY was still there on the floor of the storage room in the real world, all in one piece, no terrible wounds to her arm and shoulder. Just not breathing, and without a heartbeat. Jolene called 911, and the paramedics figured that Sam had had a heart attack, after trying to revive her. She was older, they consoled Jolene. And sometimes, no matter how healthy a person seems, their heart can go.

Jolene hadn't bothered with CPR before they arrived. She knew Sam was gone and not coming back.

Her mako sculpture had shrunk to the size of a pendant as soon as Jolene opened her eyes to the real world. Jolene pocketed it as she left the Shell Shoppe and walked across the arc of the Pier, towards the International Boardwalk area. She needed a beer something fierce.

The sun was just setting. Too many clouds for Jolene to catch a green flash, but all those clouds made for a gorgeous sunset, cirrus flames of scarlet and orange against the darkening violet sky.

And in one cloud, Jolene could just barely see her, just for a brief moment: Pele, her long dark hair flowing behind her. And a small white dog. And a slim straight figure, one hand raised in goodbye.

THE SEDUCTION OF THE SEA

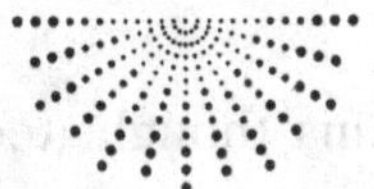

Lillian stuck her bare toes into the sea froth of the retreating wave. Goose pimples popped up on her legs and arms. The brininess of sea spray assailed her nose and she sneezed, then laughed, twirling, arms held out, beribboned straw hat in one hand. The Pacific was so lovely and wild, so unlike the slow Sacramento River.

But cold as snow melt from the High Sierras! The noonday sun, reflecting off the pale cream sand, did little to warm her, now that she'd touched the ocean.

Walking across the beach, though, that sand had nearly burned her feet, nestling in between her toes.

She'd daringly taken off her shoes and stockings before starting to the water's edge. Henry didn't care. From the sudden glint in his eyes and the quick tightening of his grip on her arm, before he let her forge ahead, she felt he approved.

Lilly wanted to please him. She was going to marry him, after all, in just two days. She should please him.

She glanced back at him over her shoulder. He was so handsome, outlined against the pines and cliffs of the cove. Slender nose, high brow, golden hair styled just so. He looked like the successful businessman that he was, even though he was only twenty seven, to her seventeen.

Though tomorrow she would be eighteen. A woman grown.

And the next day, a woman married. A frisson down her spine.

And then, babies. Henry had told her how much he wanted babies, sons and daughters both. Lillian wasn't so sure, but she wanted to make him happy. He was the only child of his parents, and though he had several cousins he was close to, he had told her how much he missed having siblings.

She was young, her mama thought too young, to marry, but her father and Henry's father wanted the match. And she loved Henry, she did. More than enough to marry him and have babies and build a home together.

An incoming eddy splashed up over her feet and up to her knees under her lace-edged cotton skirt. She could even feel the spray from the bigger waves breaking out further against the jagged rocks, dappling her bare freckled arms and sailor's blouse with tiny droplets of salty water.

The icy water was clear, clear as a mirror, and she could see rocks jutting up through the sand, and all sorts of creatures, big green anemones, brilliant orange sea stars, even an abalone, its red algae-covered shell not even hinting at the iridescence inside. She reached to touch an anemone tentacle, shrieking in laughter as she felt a tiny zap.

"Are you alright, my love?" called Henry, waiting well above the water line.

"I wonder if Mr Edison knows about these creatures," Lillian responded, brushing another tentacle. "Oh, I love the sea, Henry. I'm so glad we're spending the summer here in Carmel. I shall explore all of it!"

She focused on the rocks further out in the cove. "Oh, Henry, look! A seal!"

Indeed, a plump spotted harbor seal rested up on one of the rocks rising just a foot or two from beneath the waves, only twenty yards away from shore. The seal was watching Lillian closely, his dark brown eyes as deep and knowing as the sea itself. He barked once, then dove off the algae-slick rock, his fur darkening to charcoal in the water, his sausage-like form swift and sleek.

"He's ever so handsome," said Lillian, watching the seal surface just ten yards away. "I think I'm in love."

"Just as long as it's not more than you love me, my dear," Henry said. "Come, we must get ready for the operetta tonight. *The Fairy Shoemaker*, isn't it, at the Forest Theatre?"

Lillian reluctantly trudged back from the water's edge.

"It is," she said, brushing damp sand off her legs. "I was excited about it, but the sea itself is so much more mesmerizing."

She glanced back over her shoulder. The sea lion bobbed in the water, whiskery face intent on hers, until she reached the gravel road and got into Henry's Dodge Touring motorcar, luggage rack packed full of their trunks. With its white walled tires, burgundy leather seats, and sleek shiny black exterior, it was Henry's pride and joy. She felt like a princess in it.

But she wished she was exploring the wild Pacific, rather than bundled into Henry's luxurious motorcar.

HENRY'S PARENTS were arriving from San Francisco later that afternoon, having taken the train to Monterey, where they boarded the stagecoach to Carmel. Henry and Lillian were to meet them at the stagecoach stop, but Lillian begged off, citing her beach excursion and her need for an afternoon nap. Henry allowed that his parents were, indeed, bringing their cook, and the extra space in the car would be welcome, as he brought in their trunks.

"I'll drop Cook off at Shweninger's to pick up some provisions for a light supper," he added.

"A tin of cocoa, too, please?" Lillian asked, yawning theatrically, sneaking a look under her thick eyelashes to see if her subterfuge was working. Really, she wanted to explore the house and grounds on her own, and, if she had time, the neighborhood of little cottages. Maybe even a walk down to Ocean Avenue. And to the beach.

"Of course, my dear," Henry said as he left.

She peeked through the cream colored Belgian linen lace curtains, watching him drive off.

Alone! She tossed off her shoes and twirled on the waxed pine floors, her stockings slick against the warm smooth wood. Henry's parents were staying until a few days after the wedding, then Carmelo House, all ten rooms of it, was theirs for the summer, while Henry was employed with the La Monarca Developmental Firm, working to incorporate the town. She wasn't quite sure what Henry did specifically, but it was important enough for the firm wanted him there for the summer, and was paying for the rental of house and a small staff, which she was to hire over the next week.

The first floor consisted of a white-plastered sitting room, the kitchen with its big iron stove and lovely Mexican tiled countertops, the dining room with a ten foot long oak table, the library, and a bathroom with a toilet and sink. The upstairs, she knew, included two more bathrooms, each fully plumbed to her complete delight with soaking tubs, and three bedrooms. In two days, she would be sharing a bedroom with Henry. The thought sent chills of excitement down her spine.

The library had floor to ceiling oak bookshelves on three of the walls, packed with books and shells and cases of botanical samples and more. The fourth wall, white plastered, had a row of multi-paned windows that cranked open outward; she opened one and stuck her head out. The library overlooked a small flower garden, zinnias and dahlias and foxgloves, sandwiched between the cottage and the forest. The scent of pine and ocean mingled together pleasantly. She could see the shingled roof of another, smaller stone-clad cottage about fifty yards away through the pines. Their neighbors for the summer. She would have to introduce herself.

Plush, olive green velvet upholstered benches ran the length of the wall under the windows. She could picture herself sitting on one, reading a treatise on local sea life, while gazing out the windows ever so often. Bliss. This would be her favorite room, she knew it. Henry knew she was bookish, and loved to indulge her. She was sure he'd chosen the house based on the library itself, just for her. As a promise for the library he would one day build for her.

She exited the library, promising it she would be back soon, then went upstairs. The three bedrooms were simply furnished, each with a heavy wooden bed, carved oak armoire, and small bureau. The smooth, bleached cotton linens smelled fresh, of sunshine and lavender water. The walls were simple white plaster, like the downstairs rooms. The windows looked out onto the thick boughs of the pines. The rooms were tree houses, adrift in piney serenity, only the sweet calls of songbirds and the distant crash boom of the ocean waves breaking the silence.

She might never want to leave.

THE OPERETTA ENDED. Lillian clapped politely as she gauged the reaction of Henry and his parents. Henry looked bored, as did his father, Mr Richards. Mrs Richards, her thick brunette hair, not a streak of gray, snugged back in a tight updo, her diamonds glittering against her throat, met Lillian's regard with her own. She said nothing, just stared with her icy blue eyes.

"Did you enjoy the play, my dear?" Henry asked.

"It was lovely, thank you," Lillian responded. "But I love this—" gesturing to the piney forest which embraced the stage and seats "—far more."

The moonlight gleamed against the tops of the pines, outshining the dimming stagelights. As the perfumed and cologned theater-goers departed, the smell of the pines, tangy and sharp, and the nearby sea, salty and brisk, filled the basin of the theatre. Lillian breathed in deeply, revived. Too many people, too close, but as the crowd thinned, she relaxed.

One straggler, a tall lean man in old fashioned formal wear, caught her attention. He nodded at her as he walked by. Had she seen him before? In San Francisco, perhaps, at an opera there? Those brown eyes, deep and dark and lovely—she knew she'd seen those eyes before.

"Can we go down to the beach?" she asked, distracted. "The moonlight—"

"It's far too late," Mrs Richards cut in. "Mr Richards and I are far too tired for any more gallivanting about."

"I suppose you're right," Lillian said, crestfallen. She so wanted Mrs Richards to like her. Couldn't she see how much Lillian adored her handsome son? Lillian understood that her family was new money, her grandfather rich from timber, and Henry's was old money, from the East Coast, so much more cultured, able to trace their lineage back centuries. But the marriage had Mr Richards' approval, indeed his encouragement. He had broached the subject of marriage with *her* father, when they all had met at a function in Sacramento.

Lillian had been planning college, but then she met Henry....

"You do need your rest, my dear," Henry said. "You'll be quite busy tomorrow as well."

"I suppose," Lillian said. They filed out to the gravel road where Henry had left his motorcar. Mrs Richards and her husband sat on the spacious back seat. Lillian sat in the passenger seat, clambering up herself, ignoring Henry's hand, held out to assist her. She was quiet the entire ride back, gazing out into the piney woods, the number of cottages increasing the closer they got to Carmelo House. But the area still seemed wild and fanciful, a wood out of a fairyland.

The pale limestone walls of Carmelo House shimmered in the moonlight. Lillian's breath caught. If the stone was that lovely, what about the sand? She *was* going to the beach tonight, even if she had to sneak out and bicycle there.

"Cocoa for everyone? Lillian?" Henry asked as they all disembarked. "I'll have Cook heat up some milk."

"No, thank you," Mrs Richards said.

Lillian demurred as well. "For breakfast?" she asked.

"Of course, my dear," he said. "Whenever you like."

Mrs Richards frowned, then followed Mr Richards up the stairs. "Goodnight, Henry."

"Goodnight, mother, father. And goodnight, Lillian," he said raising her hand to his lips. "Sleep well, my love."

Lillian smiled brightly, masking her twinge of guilt. What he didn't know, wouldn't hurt. "Goodnight, Henry."

Thirty minutes later, she could hear both Mr Richards across the hall, and Henry in the bedroom next door, both snoring. She assumed Mrs Richards slept as well. The house was otherwise quiet. She quickly dressed in short wool trousers, a chemise, and a heavy wool sweater she'd knit herself. She pulled on warm wool socks as well. She'd brought her leather cycling boots with her for the summer; she'd put those on once she got outside, not wanting to risk the noise of the sturdy boots with their thick heels on the wooden stairs or floor.

Once outside, she pulled on the boots, lacing them snugly. The moon had dipped a little lower, but the gravel pathway to the garage glimmered still, little bits of feldspar and mica reflecting the soft light. The air felt thicker, saltier, stiller, and Lillian paused. Was she doing the right thing? Or just being a silly girl, indulging herself?

She scoffed. She *would* be a good wife, but she was a modern girl, and she had a mind of her own, inquisitive and bright. Enjoying the senses, the night air, the moonlight, the sea: that was all normal. And *seeing* the moonlight on the sand, dipping her toes in the water under the night sky? Maybe seeing that lovely seal once more? Magical.

The heavy wooden garage doors opened outward and were latched in the middle, a heavy wrought iron latch. She yanked it up. Henry's motorcar occupied the left and center of the garage. The bicycles were on the right, leaning up against the unfinished wooden wall. She grabbed hers and dragged it out the garage, quiet as she could, then mounted it and began her bumpy ride along the driveway, out to the road. Eyes ahead, always ahead.

So she didn't see the flicker of candlelight through the Belgian lace curtains on Mrs Richards' bedroom window.

~

TINY COTTON CANDY strands of fog toyed with the moon herself by the team Lillian reached the beach. But the sand glittered brighter than the stagelights earlier, brighter even than Mrs Richard's diamonds.

Lillian inhaled the sea air, tasted the brininess of the water, the mineral sharpness of the fog. Spray kissed her freckled cheeks, dotted her long russet eyelashes. Her thick curly auburn hair escaped from its updo and whipped around her face as the wind gusted. She unpinned it and let it fly loose.

She placed her boots and socks into the wicker basket hanging off the front handlebars. The beach was deserted this late in the evening, just her and some kelp deposited by the earlier high tide. Hers, all hers.

She heard the creaking trill of a nightjar, out hunting insects in the moonlight. The waves, crashing earlier in the day with vigor, now seemed to slide over the sand, rolling over the contours of sandbars, kissing the grains at the edge of the waterline. She walked down to the juncture of wet and dry. The dry sand, soft as fine sugar, was still warm; even the firm damp sand felt good against her bare feet, not chilly at all.

Before the engagement to Henry she had planned college, probably Berkeley, but who knew? Maybe she would go further from home, maybe even to the east coast. Or even Europe.

She wasn't quite sure what she would study: she had wanted to learn *everything*. Henry had promised he would build her a magnificent library, full of all the books she could ever want, and she had thought that would be enough.

Now, looking at the moon-kissed sea, she wasn't sure.

Well, actually, she *was* sure: sure that it wouldn't be enough, that she would always be longing for the freedom to explore, the sea, the world.

She wanted both: the library and the world.

"You should have both," a deep voice said from behind her.

She turned, unsurprised to see the lean man from the operetta. He still wore his formal wear, a decade out of date, but his long broad feet were bare like hers. He held his shoes in his left hand, and had an object—a fur, spotted and soft?—draped over his arm. His dark hair was wind-tossed and loose, not slicked back like Henry's. It looked soft, silky. His deep dark eyes stared past her, at the ocean.

"But only if you take them for yourself," he added, glancing back to her.

"I think it's too late," Lillian said quietly. "The wedding is day after, well, today, if it's past midnight."

He held out his right hand, and she clasped it in both of hers. His hand was warm; she could feel calluses, but they didn't rub unpleasantly against her skin. Rather, he just seemed more solid, more real.

And then she *saw*. Herself, radiantly pregnant; twins, a girl and a boy, with Henry's golden hair. The twins toddling about. Mrs Richards moving in to be closer to her grandchildren, her icy eyes judging Lillian every day, unceasing. Henry's growing distance as his workload increased, and her pregnant again, her eyes tired, her frame thin despite her swelling belly. A child, a son, with her auburn hair. Her face, worn, a spark of happiness when she saw her children, but that spark dulling over time as they grew and were sent off to boarding school, and there was nothing, nothing to replace them. Henry coming home late, if at all. Another pregnancy, against all hope, but this one ending prematurely, the baby miscarried... She yanked her hands away.

"It's not necessarily your future," he said. "Just a possibility."

"I don't want that," Lillian said. "It doesn't have to be like that, Henry loves me."

It was precisely what she feared. What she refused to consider.

"I'm sure he does. At least, he loves the idea of a young pretty wife, bringing a great deal of money to the marriage."

"I can't stop it."

He shrugged. "Pity. Your choice. You have the power, you just refuse to take it." His head whipped around, back to the road, a wild animal startled.

"Or maybe it won't be your choice."

She heard the crunch of tires on the gravel road, and she turned to look as well. Henry's motorcar, the top still down, with Henry driving and Mrs Richards' in the passenger seat. Her heart sank as she saw him, his handsome face tight with fury, register her, in trousers and a sweater, hair unbound, standing close to a handsome stranger. Alone, unchaperoned, on the beach, in the middle of the night.

"Come back tomorrow," the man said before Lillian trudged back across the sand. "I'll show you a different option."

Henry tied the bicycle to the luggage rack. Mrs Richards said nothing, nor did Henry, as Lillian clambered into the back seat. Henry drove them to Carmelo House, the only sound the tires on the gravel, the rumble of the engine.

"We'll discuss this in the morning," he said tightly, finally, as they entered the house.

"But—"

"In the morning."

~

LILLIAN WOKE EARLY, her head aching, dim sunlight filtering through the lace curtains. She was tired, so tired; fitful dreams had disturbed her sleep, dreams she couldn't recall, of the ocean and moonlight and running away. And now she had to face Henry and his mother.

She could hear the two of them downstairs, their voices a staccato punctuation against the bright cheeps of a songbird, the words indistinguishable. The smell of fresh bitter coffee wafted upstairs. Her stomach churned. She didn't even think she could drink cocoa, let alone coffee.

She had the wild thought of climbing out her window and running away, running to the ocean. But she knew Henry would find her. If he even bothered to look, as angry as he must be. She wasn't sure what would be worse, being found or being tossed away.

But the thought of leaving the ocean...that frightened her to her core.

She dressed quickly in her cotton skirt and sailor's blouse and stockings. Best to face the morning. She knew what she had to do.

"I don't care how much you need the funds. How much we need the settlement. She's a flighty bit of trash," Mrs Richards said as Lillian walked into the dining room and up to the table. "I've never liked her."

"She's to be my wife," said Henry. He looked at Lillian. "I was angry last night, but I do love you, my dear, and I forgive you."

"Henry, I do not deserve nor want your forgiveness," Lillian said slowly. "I'd go to the ocean again, even knowing you would catch me. I don't think I can be the wife you need me to be."

"Spoiled child," Mrs Richards said. "Seriously, Henry, do not tie yourself to this brat."

"Mrs Richards, I don't know what I did, before last night, to color you against me," Lillian said. She clutched the wooden back of the dining chair before her. "I do admit my behavior last night was inexcusable for a young woman on the eve of her marriage."

Mrs Richards sniffed.

"I imagine no woman will ever suit you for Henry," Lillian continued. "And I suspect you resent that you require the funds that I would bring through this marriage. And that resentfulness outweighs your need."

She turned to Henry. "I will procure lodging at the Pine Inn and will contact my parents. If you could bring me and my luggage there, I would be grateful."

Anger heated his eyes. "Of course," he said. To his mother: "Perhaps you are correct."

Lillian turned and went upstairs to pack.

HENRY COULDN'T DRIVE AWAY FAST ENOUGH, gravel spitting out from his tires, after hoisting her trunk off the luggage rack and setting it on the road in front of the Pine Inn on Ocean Avenue. Not a glance at Lillian, or even a quick goodbye.

"Could you post this letter to my parents, please?" Lillian asked the desk clerk as she checked in. She'd written it after she finished packing, succinctly telling her parents that the marriage was cancelled, and that she would be staying in Carmel for the summer by herself. Beyond that, she didn't know what she would do.

"Certainly," the desk clerk said, and Lillian smiled her thanks.

The Pine Inn had a lovely sun room looking towards the sea. Perhaps she could ask for something for breakfast, and have it served in the sun room, once she was unpacked. She could watch the waves. Maybe look for that dark-haired man. Maybe go out to the sea.

The bell hop wrestled her trunk up the stairs to her room. She followed slowly, trailing her hand along the warm wooden banister, her footfalls hushed by the thick navy carpet runner on the stairs. She unpacked swiftly, hanging her clothing in a carved oak armoire, then went downstairs to the sunroom.

She had a cup of cocoa and some buttered sourdough toast. She'd never tasted butter so rich, or cocoa so sweet.

A soft briny breeze fluttered the sheer cotton curtains, pushed back to either side of the windows, and teased a strand of her hair loose, tickling her cheek.

Time to go to the ocean.

The early morning fog had burned off. The sunlight glittered off the creamy sand. The water beyond shimmered a clear royal blue. The wind gusted more fiercely, more demanding, as she reached the water's edge.

She wasn't surprised to hear his deep voice again behind her.

"I truly wasn't sure you'd come back," he said as she turned to him.

"I was," Lillian said.

He held one spotted pelt over his left arm, snugged against his chest. It did look like a seal. She could see eyeholes, and limp clawed flippers dangling down.

He extended a second pelt to her.

She took the skin, marveling at its softness. "Show me," she said.

And she never looked back.

ABOUT THE AUTHOR

Since graduating from West Point, Stephannie Tallent has served in the Army as a Military Intelligence officer during Desert Storm, gotten a Zoology degree, went to vet school, worked as a small animal veterinarian, and designed and published knitting patterns and books.

Throughout all that she's always wanted to be a writer, and she's finally put all her type A, soft-spoken, invisible middle-aged woman focus on that goal, writing everything from fantasy to science fiction, mysteries and romance.

She has sold stories to Pulphouse Magazine and the WMG Holiday Spectacular.

www.stephannietallent.com

Sign up for my newsletter!
https://www.stephannietallent.com/subscribe/

ALSO BY STEPHANNIE TALLENT

Short Story Collections

Gates of Wonder

The Chronicles of Dinah Lee Wright Vol 1

The Chronicles of Dinah Lee Wright Vol 2

Gratitude of the Ocean: Jolene Tomberlin Series

The Serpent in the Shallows: Jolene Tomberlin Series

The Monkey's Journal

The Kaleidoscope Jaguars of the Jungles of Mexicatl

The Mermaid of Ellis Prime

The Alchemy of Science and Mystery

One Plus One Equals More (mystery/crime)

A Snowman Made of Sand (romance)

KnitWitch (fantasy and knitting patterns)

www.ingramcontent.com/pod-product-compliance
Lightning Source LLC
Chambersburg PA
CBHW011936050726
47590CB00011B/3323